This didn't feel like an innocent breakfast.

Jessica's senses tingled at Dan's nearness, and the scent of his cologne made her stomach swirl.

He folded his hands on top of the table. "That color looks good on you. Complements your eyes."

"Thanks." She focused on the utensils in her hands, unsure if she could handle his praise. Never before had she been so aware of him. He was Ryan's partner. His best friend. Not once had she considered him as a man. Not in the ways she had thought of him lately. Heat warmed her cheeks.

"Do I make you nervous, Jessica?"

She looked into his eyes. Big mistake. Kindness, true compassion stared back at her. "It's not that."

"What's wrong, then?" Dan cupped his hand on top of hers. Big. Strong. A hand that provided protection. One that she'd witnessed offer comfort and security to her girls. A hand she found herself yearning to feel pressed against her cheek.

"I like this…too much."

Books by Jennifer Collins Johnson

Love Inspired Heartsong Presents

A Heart Healed
A Family Reunited
A Love Discovered
Arizona Cowboy
Arizona Lawman

JENNIFER COLLINS JOHNSON

and the world's most supportive husband have been married for over two decades. They've been blessed to raise three amazing daughters and have added a terrific son-in-law. Jennifer teaches sixth-grade language arts at her local middle school. When she isn't writing or teaching, she enjoys shopping and watching movies with her family, going to dinner with her best friend and brainstorming at slumber parties with her writing buddies. She loves to hear from readers. You can reach her at jenwrites4god@bellsouth.net.

JENNIFER COLLINS JOHNSON

Arizona Lawman

HEARTSONG
PRESENTS

Recycling programs
for this product may
not exist in your area.

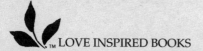 ™ LOVE INSPIRED BOOKS

ISBN-13: 978-0-373-48739-4

Arizona Lawman

Again, you have heard that it was said to the people long ago, Do not break your oath, but fulfill to the Lord the vows you have made.

—*Matthew* 5:33

This book is dedicated to my Lord and Savior,
Jesus Christ, who brings light to our darkest moments.

Chapter 1

Dan Robinson jerked to an upright position, awakened by a deep yell, followed by the smack of a phone against its base. He rubbed his eyes, blinked, then tried to focus. Raking his hand through his hair, he looked around. He'd fallen asleep at his desk. Again.

One of his fellow sergeants, an old head of the department, pulled at his striped blue tie. He unbuttoned the top of his white shirt. Thompson huffed past Dan's desk. "I've had it with her nagging. If it's not one thing, it's another."

Dan's heart twisted for the guy and his failing marriage. Seemed as though more officers were divorcing than getting married. He scratched the stubbles on his jaw. The all-night stakeout the evening before had worn him to the bone. Not deep enough to stop the recurring nightmare, though.

An unrelenting pain constricted his heart. Ryan Michaels's death haunted him, and every drug stakeout churned the memory anew. Even now, Dan didn't know the identity of the dealer who'd shot his best friend. A sketch artist had drawn the suspect's likeness, but the scumbag seemed to have vanished. Most likely he'd ripped off the wrong guy and was six feet under by now.

Dan grabbed his coffee mug and took a swig of the cold, syrupy liquid. Gagging, he scraped his tongue across his teeth. He glanced at his watch and gasped. He was late.

The chair bounced as he hopped up, and then rushed out of the police station and into his undercover car. Caught at the first light, he glanced toward the city's tennis and racquet complex. Wouldn't be as much activity there now since school had started. Mainly retired people.

Dan tapped the steering wheel, anxious for the light to change. The clock on the dash taunted him for his tardiness. The light turned green and he pushed the gas pedal, turned, then passed Surprise Stadium. Soon the building would be abuzz with Surprise Saguaros's baseball team. He turned into Ryan's neighborhood and parked several houses away from his best friend's home. *Made it.*

A garage extended from the front of the two-story stucco house. Golden eyes and brittlebushs landscaped the front of the house while Langman's sage lined the front walk. The plants had flourished since he'd helped Ryan plant them several years ago.

Within half an hour, a deliveryman arrived. A smile tugged at Dan's lips, and his pulse quickened when his deceased partner's wife accepted the package and then jumped into her van.

Since the funeral, Dan had avoided Jessica and the girls. The bullet shouldn't have hit Ryan. It should have been Dan. He had less to live for. No wife. No kids. He could easily be replaced. The promise he'd made his dying partner whirled through his mind. He shook his head and then dipped his chin. "I am watching out for them," he whispered.

Jessica had been a stay-at-home mom before Ryan's death, but now she worked three afternoons per week as the middle school lunchroom monitor. She had to work—Dan knew the benefit and insurance checks from the police department didn't cover what Ryan had made in overtime. Dan also knew the girls' soccer schedules, when Jessica went to the store, when she cleaned the house, when she had the van serviced, when she attended church. He knew it all, and in quiet ways, he made sure everything went along smoothly.

Dan gritted his teeth when his promise to Ryan seemed to peck on his skull like a woodpecker on a tree. *I am taking care of her. That's the reason I'm here.*

A burden of shame weighed his heart. His care was superficial; his promise not truly met. Ryan had never asked Dan to fall in love with his wife.

With the twist of the key, his car growled to a start. He clenched his hand into a fist and hit the passenger's seat. "I should be the one six feet under."

Jessica Michaels finished putting groceries away. Once again, she lifted a silent praise to God for the money she'd received via overnight mail delivery. Since Ryan's death, a gift of cash arrived at the beginning of each month. She always needed it. At first, she'd tried to figure out the identity of the benefactor, but when several guesses turned out to be embarrassingly wrong, she had given up the detective work and just praised God for his blessings.

Remembering that her sister planned to drop off Izzy from school, Jessica peered out the front window. Her five-year-old had begged her career-driven, lawyer/part-time professor aunt to visit her kindergarten class for show-and-tell. Kim had jumped at the opportunity to share her vast knowledge with the young minds of the future.

She and her younger sister might look alike, but that was where the similarities ended. Kim yearned to conquer the world. Jessica just wanted to spend time with her family.

A new cranberry-red Lexus convertible pulled into the driveway and parked. A blond-haired child jump out of the car, her neon-pink backpack bouncing as she ran up the walk. Jessica sucked in a breath when Kim opened the driver's door. A long silver necklace complemented an immaculate aqua two-piece skirt and shirt. High silver heels accentuated her sister's slender legs. Jessica glanced down at her own navy shorts, complete with bleach stain on the right leg. Her soiled lime V-neck T-shirt was still wet with splashes of water from loading the dishwasher. Yep, she and her sister were definitely opposites.

Forcing a smile to her lips, she opened the door and greeted Izzy with a hug. "There's my big girl. How was your day?"

"Good." Izzy wiggled away and ran into the kitchen. She pointed to the refrigerator, gripping her neck and panting. "Hurry, Mom. I need a drink."

Jessica handed her a cup of orange juice. "Dying of thirst, are we?"

"I'd have stopped and gotten her a soda, but I don't have much time before I need to be at the college," said Kim.

Which is why you didn't have to get out of the car. Jessica bit back the thought. Kim had been Jessica's greatest support since Ryan's death, but sometimes her career-driven, perfectionist sister didn't understand Jessica's desire to simply be a wife and mom.

Izzy gulped the drink, then giggled as she slammed the cup on the counter. "More, please."

Jessica tapped Izzy's nose. "I don't remember kindergarten being so strenuous when I was a girl."

"Seriously," Kim scolded. "Take a breath, Iz. Act more like a lady."

Jessica had opened her mouth to defend her daughter when the front door whammed against the wall.

"I'm telling."

"You better not."

"I'm telling."

"Maddie, I mean it." Emily grabbed Maddie's elbow.

Jessica raced to the older girls and broke them apart. "What is the matter with you two?"

"Honestly, you'd think no one has ever learned how to behave in this house," Kim mumbled.

Jessica glared at her sister before turning her attention to her older daughters.

"Maddie started it," Emily said. Tears filled the preteen's eyes. Her mouth puckered in anger. "She embarrassed me."

Maddie stuck out her tongue and chanted, "Emily and Randy sitting in a tree. K-I-S-S—"

"Stop it!" Maddie's face reddened. "See, Mom!"

Jessica turned her eight-year-old toward her. "Do not tease your sister."

Maddie shrugged and pointed to Emily. "She has a boyfriend."

Jessica raised her eyebrows and looked at Emily. "You do?"

"Mom!" Emily squealed. She clutched her books to her chest and ran up the stairs. The walls shook as her bedroom door slammed against its frame.

Kim smirked. "I don't know what the big deal is about her having a boyfriend. It's not like we didn't like boys when we were in middle school."

Jessica looked at her sister. "Because boyfriend/girlfriend pressure is not necessary in middle school."

Kim adjusted her skirt. "I'm just saying you gotta pick which battles are most important, and this one you're gonna lose."

Jessica placed her hands on her hips. "Didn't you say you needed to get to the college?"

Kim glanced at her smart phone. "Yes. One of my students wants to meet before class." She placed the phone in the front pocket of her designer purse. "But I came in to ask if you've looked through the college brochure I brought you."

Jessica pressed her lips into a firm line. Her sister had harped on her for months to go back to school, but Jessica simply didn't have the desire. "No."

Kim walked to her and pressed a perfectly manicured hand on Jessica's arm. "I just want what's best for you and the girls."

"Right now I need to take care of my daughters."

Kim released a loud sigh. "I still can't believe we come from the same parents."

My thoughts exactly.

Kim hustled to the front door. "I'll give you a call later."

Jessica rubbed her temples. She loved her sister and knew Kim meant well, but…her thoughts shifted to Emily. Not even thirteen. She was too young for boys. Looking down at Maddie, she lifted her eyebrows. "No more teasing your sister."

The eight-year-old lowered her gaze. "Okay, Mom."

At least the child appeared remorseful. Jessica lifted a quick plea to God for guidance and wished for the millionth time Ryan was still here to share the burden of parenthood. She walked into the laundry room, pulled dry clothes out of the dryer and tossed them into the laundry basket. She put wet clothes in the dryer and stuck another load in the washer.

She lifted the full basket and grunted under its weight. "It never ends." She trudged to her bedroom and started to fold a washcloth. A mess of craft material was strewn across the floor. Jessica sighed. "Izzy, please come into my room and pick up your crayons and coloring books."

"But I'm watching my favorite cartoon," Izzy's voice floated from the living room.

Jessica laid the washcloth on the bed. "No buts, young lady. Right now." Jessica heard mumbled complaints, followed by slow footsteps coming into the room.

Izzy sank to the floor and tidied up her crafts while Jessica folded the rest of the load. Finally done, she knocked softly on Emily's bedroom door.

"Go away."

"Emily, it's Mom. Let me in."

Jessica listened to the swish of bedcovers and Emily's stomps across the floor. The lock clicked and her daughter opened the door. She sauntered back to her bed and clutched a pillow to her chest. She folded her legs underneath herself like a pretzel.

"You know you can talk to me about anything." Jessica sat beside her.

Emily shrugged. She picked at the embroidered flower on her pillow sham.

Jessica brushed a stray brown curl behind her daughter's ear. The child looked so much like her father. She lifted Emily's chin to make eye contact with her. "Do you have a boyfriend?"

Emily looked away and held her pillow tighter. "It's nothing, Mom. I like Randy, and he likes me."

Jessica shifted on the bed. She twisted her diamond stud earring. "Emily, you're twelve. You have plenty of time for boyfriends. Your father and I agreed you girls would wait until high school for boyfriend-girlfriend relationships."

She wasn't ready to have this conversation with Emily. It seemed too soon. Jessica shifted again and pushed a choppy blond strand behind her own ear. She chose deliberate words. "Now, I know I can't stop you from liking a boy, but Dad and I wouldn't want you to be serious about one."

Tear-filled eyes glared at Jessica. "Well, Dad's not here, is he?" Emily tossed the pillow onto the bed and stalked toward the door. She turned and looked at Jessica. Sorrow and pain etched lines of age on her young face. "Mom, I…" Emily covered her eyes and ran into the bathroom. The lock clicked.

Jessica sat, unable to move. She couldn't decide whether to go to Emily or let her grieve. Ryan's death seemed to have been the hardest on her oldest daughter; even family counseling hadn't helped. Jessica's shoulders slumped, and she wrapped her arms around her waist. Boys and outbursts—Emily had become a different child than she'd been a year and a half ago.

Heaviness weighed her heart. "I can't do this alone, God. It's just too difficult."

Tears threatened to spill. Jessica blinked away the loathsome evidence of emotion. She lifted her shoulders and inhaled. "I have no choice."

With determination, she headed down the stairs and into the kitchen, deciding to deal with Emily later.

She pulled chicken breasts from the freezer, popped them into the microwave and pushed Defrost. Leaning against the cabinets, she took another deep breath. "There are four people in this house needing to be fed, and I'm the only one here to do it."

After a strained evening of dinner, baths and bedtime

stories and prayers, Jessica collected the dishes and put them in the sink. The doorbell rang, and she rubbed wet dishwater hands on the front of her jeans. She glanced at the clock. Past ten. Awfully late for anyone to stop by. Fear niggled at her gut as she walked toward the door.

Peeking through the peephole, she sucked in a breath. Dan Robinson? A year and a half had passed since she'd seen her husband's old partner.

Her heartbeat raced and a smile lifted her lips as she opened the door. *Wow. He looks great.* Short, dark brown hair, matching scruffy mustache and beard accompanied by piercing blue eyes.

When their eyes met, the corners of his mouth turned up slightly just the way they used to when he was uncertain of something. She giggled at the realization of how much she had missed him. "Get in here, Woolly Mammoth. You're blocking the moonlight in my doorway."

She chuckled when his old nickname escaped her lips. The man had to be the biggest guy on Surprise's police department, if not the whole state of Arizona.

Dan's expression registered wonder. "No one's called me that in a long while." A slow grin of pleasure trailed his words.

Tears filled Jessica's eyes as memories washed over her. She squeezed Dan's hand and blinked. "It's good to see you." She released his hand and opened her arms wide. "I could use one of your old hugs."

She saw fear flash through Dan's eyes before he nodded. Pulling her into a bear hug, he lifted her off her feet and twirled her around until she felt dizzy. Soft giggles escaped her as he placed her on her feet. She closed her eyes and sighed. "That's the best I've felt in a long time."

"I need to talk to you, Jessica." She opened her eyes

and noticed Dan's hands shoved in his pockets. He stared at his shuffling feet.

She grabbed his arm. "Let me get you a drink. Do you still like Coke?"

"Yeah. Thanks."

She led him to the kitchen. Dan plopped into a seat at the table and folded his hands in front of him.

Jessica placed an ice-filled glass of soda on the table. "So, what do you need to talk to me about?"

"Emily."

Fear mounted in Jessica's heart. Her eldest daughter struggled more each day. She was like a volcano ready to erupt. Jessica lowered herself into a chair. "What about her?"

Chapter 2

Dan took a deep breath and peered into Jessica's intense blue eyes. *Lord, this woman hurts me.* Never did he have any intention of spending time with her. His attraction for her jabbed at his loyalty to his friend. If Dan's teenage informant hadn't told him about Emily's boyfriend, he would have kept his distance.

"Please. Tell me." Jessica placed her hand on his.

Electricity shot through his veins and into his heart. He looked at the small hand atop his. Her skin was dry, even cracked in a few places, yet her hands were beautiful. Long fingers made way for small, perfect, natural pink fingernails. The dryness displayed her devotion to seeing to the needs of her family, which only attracted him more. *Stop it,* he groaned inwardly, and tore his gaze from her hand and looked at his Coke. "Did you know Emily has a boyfriend?"

"Maddie mentioned it. I talked to Emily today and

told her I didn't want her in a boy-girl relationship." She frowned, her fine features drooping in concern. "Why? What's going on?"

He gulped as he found himself drowning in her gaze. "The boy Emily likes—Randy Mullins. He…" What should Dan say? He couldn't reveal any confidential information. "He's not the best kid for Emily."

Jessica narrowed her gaze. "What do you mean?"

"He's not safe."

Jessica's eyebrows lifted, and she bit her bottom lip. "They're in eighth grade. He can't be that bad. Not alcohol or drugs, or…"

Dan furrowed his brow and released a sigh. He didn't respond, but Jessica's eyes widened; she'd read his expression as he'd intended. She crossed her arms on the table. "I don't know what to do. She's so rebellious. I feel like I'm losing her."

Dan flinched at her pain. He longed to stroke her hair and whisper promises of protection and help in her ear. Shaking the nonsense from his thoughts, he balled his fists and sat stiff in his seat. *Remember who she belongs to.*

Jessica lifted her gaze to meet Dan's. "Will you help me? Maybe she'll talk to you. She's so angry about Ryan's death. She needs a man's influence." Jessica placed her hand atop his. "Please, Dan. Help me?"

Dan melted like an ice cube in a pot of boiling water. *I promise.* The last words he'd uttered to his best friend and partner replayed in his mind. He shifted in his chair and took a long drink of soda. Swallowing hard, he grinned halfheartedly at Jessica's hopeful expression. "Of course I'll help you."

Jessica jumped out of her chair and threw her arms around Dan's neck. *Woman, you're going to have to quit doing that*. He unwrapped Jessica's arms from around him. "When and where do you want me?"

Jessica glanced toward her refrigerator, then looked at her watch. "Tomorrow is Friday. Can you believe we don't have any soccer practices?"

"I know."

"Huh?"

"Never mind." Dan took another quick drink. "When can we meet?"

"Why don't you come for supper, and we'll talk to Emily afterward? Oh, Dan." Jessica grabbed his hand and squeezed. "The girls will be so happy to see you."

Later that night, Dan tossed and turned. He didn't sleep a wink. The next day he simply went through the motions at work. His thoughts tormented him—he should have looked after Jessica and the girls better. If only his heart hadn't been so weak.

Time sped and slowed until he found himself at her front door again. He adjusted the collar of his button-down shirt and rang the bell. He pressed his car key between each of his fingers, calming his nerves with the coolness of the metal. "I can do this. I can do this. I can do this."

The door swung open and a small blond-haired child latched on to his leg. "Uncle Woolly, it's really you." Izzy rubbed her cheek against his jeans and purred. "I missed you, Uncle Woolly. Am I still your little kitty?"

Guilt overwhelmed him as he lifted her into his arms. *I should have been a physical part of their lives this past year and a half.* He squeezed her to his chest. "Izzy, you'll always be my little kitty."

"Uncle Woolly, Uncle Woolly." Maddie plummeted through the open door and wrapped her arms around his waist. She nestled her face into the belly of his shirt, then lifted her gaze to look at him. "You smell like Uncle Woolly."

Dan laughed. "Is that good or bad?"

"Good."

Jessica came to the door and grinned. She crossed her arms and leaned against the frame. "Are you going to stand on my porch all night?"

And there's the reason I've stayed away. Dan quickly gazed at her perfect figure-eight shape. *How in the world has that woman borne three kids?* Shaking away his wayward thoughts, he looked down at one child wrapped around his waist and the other around his neck. He cocked his head to the side. "I'm not sure I can move."

Jessica laughed and motioned her daughters into the house. "Come on, girls. You can each sit beside him at the dinner table."

"Yay!" they squealed in unison. Dan placed Izzy on the ground. She and Maddie ran into the house.

Dan looked up to find Jessica staring at him. She grinned slightly. "Dan, the girls missed you." She motioned him inside. "I'm so glad you're here."

Clutching his keys tightly in his palm, he walked into the house. He hadn't been in Jessica's presence more than five minutes and already he felt weak in the knees and sick to his stomach. Trying to focus on the reason for his visit, he asked, "Where's Emily?"

"In her room. She knows why you're here, and she's not happy about it." Jessica placed one hand on the stairs' banister. "Emily, it's time to come down. Dinner's ready."

A door shut. Dan watched as the young lady teetering between child and adult sauntered down the stairs. *This is the age when a girl needs her daddy.*

She reached the bottom step and Dan placed his arm around her shoulder. "How's it going, kiddo?"

Angry eyes glared up at him as she shrugged away from his grip. "I'm not a kid anymore."

Dan lifted both hands in surrender. "Okay, okay." He touched her chin with his thumb. "You're right, Emily. You've grown into a beautiful young lady."

Emily blushed and looked away from him. Without a word, he guided her toward the dining room.

"Your admirers await." Jessica pointed at the grinning girls sitting on each side of an empty chair.

Pain laced Dan's heart. *I guess girls of all ages need their daddies.*

Dan sat between Izzy and Maddie and tousled each of their hair. "I haven't felt this popular in a long time."

He looked around the once-familiar room. The joined kitchen and dining area was still painted in dust-bowl brown and decorated with a fruit-wallpaper border. Country wood pieces and pictures adorned the walls. The oak china cabinet still held Jessica's grandmother's dishes, and stacks of bills and notes were still piled on Ryan's antique desk.

As a stay-at-home mom, Jessica had always kept her house in tiptop shape, or at least she had when Ryan was alive. Dan couldn't help noticing one of the kitchen cabinets was missing a handle, and several places on the walls needed some serious touch-up. Even his chair wobbled beneath him.

There's no telling what needs fixed that I can't see. Jessica could have used a husband these past eighteen months. Why, God? Why did you take Ryan? It should have been me.

Izzy tapped his hand with the end of her fork. "Don't you like lasagna?"

Dan looked at her and smiled. "I love lasagna." He cut

off a huge bite from the piece on his plate and shoveled it into his mouth. "Mmm, mmm, mmm."

He closed his eyes and shook his head. "Your mommy makes the best lasagna in the whole world." Dan speared another large piece onto his fork and shoved it into his mouth. "Mmm."

Izzy scrunched her nose and giggled. "You're funny, Uncle Woolly."

Dan wiped tomato from his mouth and took a drink of soda.

He looked across the table at Emily. She snarled her nose and twisted her fork around her untouched plate. He glanced at Jessica. She hadn't eaten, either. She stared at her oldest daughter—helplessness written all over her face.

God, help me here. I don't know how to get through to Emily.

Izzy laid her hand on his forearm and scooted her chair closer to his. "Uncle Woolly, will you come to my soccer game tomorrow?"

Dan looked into her pleading eyes. "Well, I…"

Maddie grabbed his other arm. "Oh, and you can come to mine, too. Please, please, please."

Dan glanced at Maddie, who pushed a long blond strand of hair off her face and stuck out her bottom lip. "Well, I…"

"Girls." Jessica glared at the twosome. "Dan may have other plans tomorrow. Where are your manners?"

"Aunt Kim says we don't have any," Emily growled.

Izzy and Maddie released him and lowered their heads.

Dan thought his heart would break. He wrapped his arms around their shoulders and nestled them to him. "Of course I'll go. When do the games start?"

"Mine's at ten," Maddie yelled.

"And mine's at eleven," Izzy hollered.

Dan looked across the table at Jessica. She shook her head. "You don't have to do this," she said.

He winked. "I want to."

"Izzy, Maddie," Jessica addressed her younger daughters, "I want you two to run upstairs and start your baths."

Izzy slouched and slammed her napkin on the table. "Aw, do we have to?"

Jessica snapped her fingers and pointed toward the stairs. "Yes. Go."

Izzy and Maddie stood and slouched away from the table. Emily stood, as well.

"You stay," Jessica commanded.

Emily huffed and slithered back into her chair. "Go ahead and tell me you don't like Randy." She practically spit the livid words at Dan. "I don't care what you think."

"Emily, you will not talk to an adult—"

Dan lifted his hand to stop Jessica. "You know what, Emily, I haven't been part of your life, and you're right to feel you don't want me to intrude." He glued his gaze to hers. "But I must. Randy Mullins is not a boyfriend you should have."

Emily peered at him, then shrugged. "I still like him."

She was challenging him, and he intended to meet her on it. "Why?"

"Why what?"

"Why do you like him?"

She crossed her arms and leaned back in the chair. "He's cute, and I don't care what he does."

Dan glanced at Jessica. She sat straight as a statue, all emotion gone from her face. He stared at Emily for several seconds. "I think you do care."

Surprise registered on the young girl's face, and she lowered her eyes. Dan reached across the table and grabbed her hand. "You're a good girl, Emily. And you're a Christian. You love God, and you know what is right."

Tears filled her eyes. She sniffed.

Jessica wrapped her arm around Emily's shoulder. "You're precious, honey. I don't want you to go with this boy."

Emily flinched from her mother's touch. "You don't understand." She jumped and ran up the stairs.

Jessica stood.

Dan grabbed her hand. "Let her go. She's struggling."

"How can you be so nonchalant about this?"

"I saw it in her eyes. She's fighting God, but she's losing."

Fear etched Jessica's face. "I pray you're right." Determination and anger took over her expression. "'Cause, if you're not I'll…I'll…"

Dan knew Jessica couldn't think of what she'd do to Emily. A sudden fire lit her eyes. She pushed her shoulders back and flipped a stray curl from her face. Getting Jessica riled was a feat, but once she reached her breaking point… He'd hate to be the one who crossed her.

He scratched at his short beard. Nah, he'd like it. Passionate fury could expose a burning, all-consuming love. *Stop it.* He shook his head, stood and then stacked up the dishes. "Can I help you do these before I go?"

Jessica exhaled. Dan watched as anger slipped from her face and was once again replaced with worry. She rose on tiptoes and kissed his cheek. "No, just go."

His skin burned. He should insist on helping with the dishes…. He glanced into bright blue eyes, a spiraling hurricane of love and anger for her child. Her caring nature attracted him like a moth to light. Longing gripped him. No, he couldn't stay. He had to get out of here—and fast.

Slipping his keys out of his front pocket, he jingled them

in his hand and headed for the door. "Thanks for dinner, Jessica. Guess I'll see you tomorrow." Dan looked above her head, to the side, at the floor—anywhere but her face.

"Thanks for your help, Dan." Jessica followed him and opened the door. "You just can't imagine how much I appreciate it."

"It's nothing." He waved quickly, then bolted out of the house for his car. *Whew. That was close. There is no way I could handle another hug from that woman.*

Jessica tightened the belt of her fluffy ivory robe. She grabbed a clip, twisted her hair in a knot and secured the longer strands in place. Exhausted, she grabbed her Bible, a sketch pad and a pencil, then trudged down the stairs and into the kitchen. She pulled a package of hot cocoa from the cabinet and laid it on the counter. Selecting her favorite MOM mug from the dishwasher, she filled it with water and placed it in the microwave for two minutes.

As the water warmed, Jessica glanced around her home. She hadn't entertained anyone since Ryan's death. So many things needed to be fixed; painting and deep cleaning were only the superficial things. She dared not think about leaky faucets, broken light fixtures, nicks in the baseboards and the hole in the living room wall from Izzy's accidental slip on roller skates.

The microwave beeped and she popped open the door. She dumped the contents of a hot cocoa packet into the mug and stirred the mixture. Jessica licked the spoon, her chest tight—in the past, she would have stirred two mugs while Ryan teased how they were the only couple in Arizona who enjoyed a late-night hot cocoa after a long day of desert heat. She fell into a dining room chair and it cracked beneath her weight.

"Add broken chair to the list." She lifted her finger and

checked an imaginary list titled Things That Need to be Fixed Since Ryan Died.

Her house exemplified her life—only halfway done. She was a halfway decent mom, housekeeper, cook and lunchroom monitor. She was even a halfway decent Christian. If her sister had her way, Jessica would also be a halfway decent college student.

She placed the mug on the table and opened the drawing pad. Dreams of art school flashed through her mind. She'd never intended to make a career of her art, but she wanted to learn more about shades and shapes and designs. She used to think maybe she'd design greeting cards or calendars to make a little extra money for the family. Art was her passion. Having married and started their family so young, she and Ryan agreed she'd wait until Izzy began kindergarten for Jessica to take a few classes.

"Well," she started. Jessica opened the pad to a clean sheet. "I didn't."

She picked up the pencil and drew a round shape. The page came to life as a face formed. Scratchy motions produced facial hair. Kind eyes soon developed. She shaded below the cheekbone. A firm, square jaw appeared.

"It's Dan."

Surprise welled within her. She'd never sketched anyone but Ryan and the girls in this book. This was her family pad. Part of her wanted to rip the page from the binding. Gentle eyes peering back at her refused the action.

He fit there. On that very page.

Determined not to overanalyze it, Jessica closed the pad and lifted the mug to her lips. Her body warmed as she sipped the cocoa.

As she glanced at the Bible, God's Word seemed to beckon. She picked it up and flipped through pages.

"Where is that rest verse? That's what I'd like to read." She thumbed through Matthew before settling on chapter 11.

"Ah. Here it is."

Jessica read aloud. "'Come to Me, all you who are weary and burdened, and I will give you rest.'"

She closed the Bible and recited the verse from memory. "God, I need that verse pasted in big letters on my forehead." She chuckled. "Wonder what Emily would think of that."

Groaning, she rubbed her temples. The past year and a half had been a spiraling gyro. Everything she said, Emily misconstrued. Jessica had no idea how to handle her almost teenage daughter. She glanced at the family portrait on the wall. "What will she be like when she actually *is* a teenager?" she mumbled.

After Ryan's death, Emily had been quiet and reserved. Wouldn't open up. Not even to cry. Jessica and the girls had gone to counseling. Even there, Emily refused to talk. A month passed, and Emily became clingy. Jessica couldn't walk into another room without Emily by her side. Izzy and Maddie adjusted to life without their daddy, but then Emily cried—a lot.

Again, Jessica had sought counseling. That time Emily had opened up, sharing her fears of losing her mom and sisters, and her own fears of death. Emily was afraid her daddy would forget her in heaven. She felt guilty she hadn't hugged him before he went to work that night. Several months of counseling had helped, and soon Emily rejoined life. She didn't cry every moment, didn't cling to Jessica as if her life depended on it.

The past few months had brought about a new change, though. Emily had become obstinate, confrontational and even downright disrespectful. Jessica had tried to be patient, but lately she felt weary and fearful to the depths of her spirit. Emily's attitude had become so coarse. Jessica closed her eyes.

Rest.

Yes. I must rest. Jessica stared at the ceiling. "God, I can't take these burdens. They're too heavy for me. I'm giving them to You in exchange for that rest. It's an unfair trade, I know. But You offered."

Jessica grinned, collected her things and strode up the stairs. Her covers begged her to join them. She set her alarm clock for six o'clock and snuggled between the sheets. She envisioned herself a small babe in the palm of her Heavenly Father's right hand. He snuggled her against His chest. She exhaled a sigh of release. At this moment, she was safe resting in His arms.

Chapter 3

Izzy ran toward Dan with a juice box in one hand and gummies in the other. "Uncle Woolly, did you see me score a goal?"

"I saw it. You were great!" Dan squatted and hugged her. "How 'bout I treat you girls to a hamburger and fries?"

"Will you really?" Maddie's voice sounded behind him. She had been dribbling the soccer ball with her feet across the sidelines. She wiped sweat off her brow with the back of her hand.

"Sure." He tousled her damp hair. Not even noon yet and the hot Arizona sun already beat down on them. An oversize sweet tea sounded downright delicious. He glanced at Jessica. She was engrossed in a private conversation with Emily. The preteen stood stiffly beside her mother, looking at Jessica, but obviously not listening.

"Jessica." Dan broke up the conversation. "I'd like to treat you girls to lunch. How does a hamburger sound?"

She walked toward him, waving her hands in front of her chest. "Girls, you must stop this. You cannot invite someone to take you to lunch." She stopped inches away from Izzy and Maddie and placed her hands on her hips. "Surely, I've taught you better than this."

Both girls' expressions dropped, and Dan insisted, "They didn't ask. I offered. They played hard, and they deserve a treat."

Izzy and Maddie looked up, eagerly awaiting their mother's verdict.

Remorse crossed Jessica's features. "Thank you, Dan. I'm…I'm sorry, girls."

"That's okay." Izzy skipped away, then turned toward her sister. "Maddie, I'll race you to the car." She took off in a dead sprint toward the minivan.

"No fair." Maddie ran behind.

Emily wrinkled her nose, then rolled her eyes as she dragged her feet toward the vehicle. Jessica stood beside him, shoulders slouched and expression drawn. His heart constricted. Once again, he longed to wrap her small frame in his arms. He might not be able to protect her from everything, but he'd sure take care of as many things as possible. He grabbed his keys from his front pocket and clutched the cool metal between his fingers.

Jessica bent to pick up two bagged folding chairs. Dan scooped them up and hefted them over his shoulder. "Let me help you."

"Thanks." Her voice snapped like a lion tamer's whip. She rubbed her forehead. "I'm sorry, Dan. I'm worried about Emily."

Her vulnerability played tricks on his heart. Shoving his emotions to the side, he placed his arm around Jessica's shoulder. "Let's not think about it right now. I'm starving. How 'bout you?"

Jessica nestled closer to him as they walked to the van. *Oh. Woman, you must not do that.*

She looked up at him and grinned. "You're right. Let's eat."

At the fast-food restaurant, Dan shoved the last bite of cheeseburger into his mouth and maneuvered a bit away from the clinging five-year-old. He enjoyed the doting Izzy; however, breathing proved a necessary part of life.

Izzy slithered closer to him again and wrapped her arms around his waist. "Uncle Woolly, will you come to my school tomorrow for show-and-tell?"

Emily grunted. "Tomorrow's Sunday, dummy."

Jessica plopped her napkin onto the table. "Do not call your sister that."

Emily pursed her lips and stared at the ceiling.

Jessica faced her youngest daughter. "Your show-and-tell is on Friday, but Uncle Woolly works. I'm sure it's not easy—"

"Please, will you come?" Izzy squeezed his arm tighter and stuck out her bottom lip. "Please, please, please."

Boy, she's a pro. How's a guy supposed to turn down this little one?

"Izzy," Jessica reprimanded. "That's enough."

Dan chuckled and nestled her under his arm. "I'd love to go. Jessica, what time do I need to be there?"

Jessica placed a French fry back in its carton and wiped her hands with a napkin. "You don't have to do this. These girls act like they've never been taught manners when they're around you."

Emily huffed. "I'm not acting like them."

Jessica glared at her, but he tapped his watch to shift her attention back to him. "What time?"

"Her show-and-tell is at one o'clock."

He wadded his trash in a ball, placed it on the tray and

then kissed the top of Izzy's head. The girls had lost their manners around him because he never should have left. "I wouldn't miss it for the world."

Emily walked down the stairs Monday morning before school. Taking in the short denim skirt and sparkly green eye shadow, Jessica blinked several times, sure her eyes were deceiving her. When the vision didn't change, she planted both hands on her hips. "Just what do you think you're wearing?"

Emily snorted. "I'm not thinking. The clothes are on my body."

Jessica balled her fist and pressed it against her lips. The urge to march her back up the stairs and wash out the snide comments with soap nearly overwhelmed her. But she determined not to act in anger, and instead to discipline without regrets. Releasing a slow breath, she extended her open palm to the twelve-year-old. "Phone."

Emily's jaw dropped, and she shook her head. "I'm sorry, Mom. I won't talk to you like that."

Though Emily's pleading expression tugged at Jessica's heartstrings, she'd been lenient with the girl for too long. "Sorry won't cut it. Give me the phone."

A tear slid down Emily's cheek as she tugged the old flip phone from her front pocket. "Just for the day, right?"

The front door opened, and the click of heels tapped against the tile floor. Kim whistled. "Not sure that attire will pass dress code, Em."

Jessica focused on her daughter as she closed her hand around the phone. She'd be sure to check everything on it before giving it back to the defiant child. "No. A week."

"Mom!" Emily screeched.

Kim covered her ears with both hands. "Whoa. Why don't we talk about this?"

Ignoring her sister, Jessica touched the bottom of the skirt. "Didn't we put this away for Maddie...two years ago? And where, may I ask, did you get that makeup?"

Jessica tapped her foot against the hard floor. Emily had better come up with a good explanation. A costume party. Something. Cinderella's stepsisters could take a backseat to her brewing anger.

Emily swiped away her tears and jutted out her jaw. "The makeup came from a friend. She's letting me borrow it."

Kim touched Jessica's arm. "I could take her to my cosmetologist. She could show Emily how to properly apply eye shadow. She's getting older and—"

"No," Jessica interrupted. She glared at Emily. "You will give the makeup back. Today."

"The awful green eye shadow needs to go," Kim said, "but she is getting older, and—"

Jessica turned to her sister. "I said no."

Kim lifted smooth manicured hands up in surrender. "Fine. I just came to get Maddie. It's her turn for breakfast."

Jessica swallowed down the guilt that now mingled with her rage. Her sister had come to the rescue more times than she could count since Ryan's death. Despite her fashion-forward, career-driven ways, she loved her nieces. "I'm sorry, Kim."

Kim winked, then yelled, "Maddie, you ready?"

Maddie raced down the steps with Izzy following fast on her heels.

"I wanna go, too," Izzy whined.

Kim cupped her chin. "Next week is your turn."

Izzy scrunched her nose and crossed her arms in front of her chest. "It's not fair."

Maddie bobbed her head. "Is too fair."

"That's enough, girls." Jessica nudged Izzy's back. "Your breakfast is on the table."

Izzy stomped to the kitchen while Maddie put on her backpack. She frowned at Emily. "What happened to your eyes?"

Jessica narrowed her gaze at her oldest daughter. "Nothing a little soap won't fix."

Kim cleared her throat. "On that note, Maddie and I will be leaving."

Emily walked up two steps. "I'll just put it on once I get to school."

Fury rushing inside her once again, Jessica marched to her child. "No, you won't. You must have forgotten I work at your school. If I see even a speck of green on your eyes, I promise everyone in that school will know it."

Emily's bottom lip quivered and tears welled in her eyes anew.

Determined to stand her ground, Jessica pointed to her palm. "And you will bring that skirt downstairs and place it in my hand."

Emily raced up the stairs, and Jessica prayed for strength and wisdom as the child's sobs tore at her resolve. Joining Izzy in the kitchen, she poured a mug of coffee and then sat beside her youngest.

"Mom, what's wrong with Emily?"

Jessica patted Izzy's hand. "She's mad at me."

Izzy lifted her eyebrows and spread her arms wide. "She's always mad."

"I know." Jessica kissed Izzy's head, then bit her bottom lip to keep her emotions under control. She and Ryan had said the girls couldn't wear makeup until high school, but maybe Kim was right. Lots of middle school girls wore makeup, and if Emily learned how to apply it properly… She sighed. *God, I want You to speak in an audible voice and tell me the right parenting decisions. Being a mom has never been easy, but when Ryan was here I had someone to help set up rules, an ally...*

"Here, Mom."

Jessica turned at the sound of Emily's shaky voice. Makeup free, Emily held the denim skirt extended in her right hand, her big blue eyes sad and sorry.

Jessica took the skirt and placed it on the table. "I love you. I always want what's best for you."

Emily didn't answer. She looked at her feet, then walked to the front door.

Jessica had no idea how to handle her daughter—ground her, love her. *Right now I'll show her I love her.* She went to Emily and wrapped her in an embrace.

Emily stood still for a moment, then wiggled away. "Izzy and I need to get to the bus stop."

Jessica kissed Emily's forehead. "I love you, Emily."

"Okay. Bye, Mom."

Chapter 4

Dread filled Dan as he opened the double doors of the Early Childhood Center. What did he know about little kids? He'd always cared for Ryan's girls. Had even been coerced to change a diaper on one of them. But a whole school of four- and five-year-olds? A shiver trailed his spine. He hoped he didn't accidentally squash one.

He glanced to his left and right. No little munchkins running the halls, though their work splattered the bright green-and-blue walls in the form of paintings, drawings, letters and math papers. He lifted his eyebrows at a few of the stories; he'd never dreamed little kindergartners could write so much.

Dan adjusted the gun belt higher on his waist. After years of wearing regular clothes for undercover work, he was anything but comfortable in his police uniform. But he'd worn it for Izzy, figuring the kids would want to see his handcuffs, nightstick and the like.

Looking down the halls on both sides again, he scratched his stubbly jaw. *How's a guy supposed to know where to go? Not an office sign in sight.* He peeked into the door on his right. No one there.

Irritation welled within him. Now that he thought about it, he shouldn't be wandering the hall looking for the office. Those front doors should have been locked. In today's times, there was no telling who might walk into a school with bad intentions. Safety should be a school's number one priority. As soon as he found the office, he'd be sure to have a word with the principal.

"May I help you, Officer?"

Dan spun around and stared at an attractive brunette. "I'm…looking for the office."

She smiled, lowered her eyelashes. "I'll show you the way. Here for show-and-tell?"

"Yes. Miss Stephens's class."

A smile as mischievous as the Cheshire cat's in *Alice in Wonderland* lifted her lips. He followed the woman down the hall and to the left. She pointed to a glass door marked Office. She looked at his left hand and smiled. "Here you are. Hope to see you around."

Straightening his shoulders, he puffed out his chest. The woman had to be a decade younger than him. Quite a beauty, too. His squad of twenty-something officers liked to tease him about being single and pushing forty, even though he was only thirty-six. And maybe he wouldn't be single if he hadn't fallen for his best friend's widow.

Pushing away the thought, he entered the office. Dan noted the look of disgust on the middle-aged woman's face.

"Can I help you?" the receptionist's voice croaked like a frog.

"Yes." He placed his elbow on the desk. "But first, did

you realize the front doors are unlocked? Someone must have forgotten—"

Giving him a deadpan expression, the woman shook her head. "They're locked."

Annoyance swelled within him, and he stood up straight. "I just walked in. They're unlocked."

Her blank look didn't change as she pointed to the monitor behind her desk. "I saw you and unlocked them." She tapped a button on the wall, then looked at him as if he had the intelligence of a cactus. "Electronically."

Dan narrowed his gaze. "I could have been an intruder."

"You're wearing a police uniform."

"That doesn't mean I'm an actual officer."

"You arrested my son last week."

Dan stepped back. He thought she looked familiar, but he couldn't quite place her. It explained her rude demeanor, though. Quite a few people had gotten mad at him when he caught their family member doing something illegal.

She frowned. "What do you need?"

"I'm here for Izzy Michaels. I don't know her teacher…."

"Yeah, you do."

Dan furrowed his eyebrows. He'd just about had it with the woman's rude attitude. He was not to blame that her son chose to break the law. "No. I'm pretty sure I don't."

"She just brought you to my desk. Her name is Miss Stephens." The older woman emphasized the word *Miss*. "That girl will throw herself…" The secretary mumbled the rest of her sentence.

"Excuse me?" Dan peered at the older secretary. He remembered her now. Her son had sold drugs to one of his undercover guys, and she'd thrown a fit when his officer arrested him.

She cleared her throat and pointed to the clipboard on

her desk. "Are you checking Izzy out? 'Cause you can't if you're not on her emergency list."

"No. I'm here for show-and-tell."

"Of course," she mumbled.

"What was that?"

"Nothing. Sign your name and place a visitor sticker on your shirt. Miss Stephens is in Room 20."

"Thanks," Dan grunted, and left before he said something he'd later regret.

He ambled a few steps down the hall. Hesitantly, he glanced through the window looking for Izzy. She spotted him and waved. Running to the door, she opened it wide. Her hand wrapped around his index finger and she pulled him into the room. "Miss Stephens, this is my uncle Woolly. He's my show-and-tell."

Rich chocolate-drop eyes stared up at him. She batted her eyelashes. "So we meet again…Uncle Woolly." She purred his nickname, and then patted Izzy's head. "I ran into him on the way to pick up the class from art." She looked back at him and winked.

That was definitely flirting, and a bit too strong for his liking. Dan forced his lips into a smile and turned to Izzy. "Where do I sit?"

Izzy tightened her grip and dragged him to the carpeted area. "Right there." She pointed to one of the many X's forming a circle on the carpet.

"Here's a chair for you, Uncle Woolly," cooed Miss Stephens as she placed a folding chair on the spot.

"Thank you, and my name is Dan Robinson."

She batted her eyelashes again, but he ignored her and glanced around at the kids. Some wore expressions of awe, at either his uniform or his size. Others seemed terrified. He sat, and Izzy threw herself into his lap. "I sit here."

He hugged her to his chest. She'd really grown on him

this past week. Her never-ending love was just what a grumpy ole bachelor needed.

Miss Stephens flitted toward the circle and invited the children to grab their items and sit on an *X*. Dan was all too aware of her constant gaze as each child collected his or her individual treasure and found a spot on the floor.

Izzy volunteered to go last because her prized possession was a real person. Dan listened as the kids relayed stories about the treasures they'd brought to school.

After the last child finished sharing, Izzy's teacher looked at Dan and winked. "It's your turn, Izzy."

Miss Stephens lowered her eyelids. The corners of her mouth lifted in a sly grin. Dan cleared his throat. *She's flirting in front of a bunch of five-year-olds.*

Izzy stood and pointed to him. "This is Uncle Woolly. He's my daddy's best friend. My daddy died at work, but Uncle Woolly was with him making him feel better. He came to my soccer game on Saturday and took us out for lunch. He's the best." She wrapped her arms around his neck and squeezed. "I love him."

Shame overpowered him. "I love you, too, sweetheart."

Ryan's girls needed a man in their lives. He had promised his friend to watch out for them. Sure, he sent money each month, but that wasn't all they needed. They needed attention and affection, things he should have been willing to give them all along. *They'll have it now.*

The bell rang. Dan gave Miss Stephens the letter from Jessica stating he would take Izzy home.

She smiled. "And here's a letter for Mrs. Michaels about the upcoming fall festival." Miss Stephens placed the paper in Dan's hand and allowed her fingers to linger.

Dan shoved the paper in his pocket, then took Izzy's hand. "I'll be sure she gets it."

He bolted for the door. An invisible hook seemed to

grab his collar. He loosened the top button. He had the most overwhelming feeling this woman was trying to reel him in.

After the evening services, Maddie and Izzy raced to the fenced-in playground behind the church. Jessica held the new youth materials to her chest as she made her way downstairs to the youth center. As secretary for the Sunday-school department, she had a legitimate excuse to invade Emily's domain. Her daughter couldn't fuss at Jessica for doing her job. She wrinkled her nose. The child *shouldn't* fuss, but she most likely would. Everything Jessica did made the almost-thirteen-year-old mad.

Contemporary Christian music boomed from speakers as she opened the door to the large room that had once been the church's fellowship hall. Over the years, the congregation had grown so much the church had built onto the existing sanctuary and education building, allowing the students to use the area, which even included a fully furnished kitchen.

One of the older boys stood in front of the group leading the song. Jessica spied Emily near the front sitting with a group of students her age. Her face shone as she belted out the lyrics to the praise song. Jessica's heart warmed, and she thought of how Mary tucked in her heart Simon's and Anna's words about her son, Jesus. When Emily challenged her again in the coming days, weeks and years, Jessica prayed God would remind her of this moment: a time when she saw her child's honest and complete praise.

"Those for me?"

Jessica jumped at the sound of Valerie Dean's voice.

The woman chuckled. "Didn't mean to scare you."

Jessica handed the books to her pastor's wife. "Shouldn't have scared me. I was just focusing on the kids."

"Good to see your child praising the Lord, isn't it?"

Jessica released a long breath and blinked several times when sudden tears welled in her eyes. "You have no idea."

Valerie furrowed her brow and nodded her head toward a small room at their right. "Let's talk a minute."

Jessica dabbed the moisture from the corners of her eyes and followed the older woman into the room. "I'm fine. Just a little emotional."

Valerie shut the door. "You know I know better. Let's hear it."

Jessica looked around the room, which served as the middle school girls' Sunday-school room. The very place Emily had been only an hour ago. She shrugged. "It's just hard sometimes."

"Being a mother who has a caring, involved husband is hard. Being a widow with three girls would be impossible." Valerie shook her head. "Even with their daddy in the house, there were days I didn't think I'd survive when our four girls were teenagers."

Jessica chin quivered. "Emily can be difficult at times."

Valerie pulled a tissue out of the box and handed it to Jessica. "Spill it."

A dam of emotions broke from Jessica's chest, and she told Valerie everything. She shared about the boy from Emily's school, how she didn't even know how bad the boy was because Dan hadn't told her much. She told her about Emily's makeup-and-apparel shenanigans, and her fear that maybe she was holding on to Emily too tight. She talked about soccer games and homework and upcoming fall festivals. By the time she took a breath, her heart ached from the confusion she felt.

Valerie chewed her bottom lip and didn't say a word. Embarrassment niggled at Jessica—she'd just unloaded more frustration and emotion than she had since Ryan's death.

"Who's this Dan guy?"

Jessica frowned. "What?"

"When you were talking, you kept mentioning some guy named Dan."

Jessica clasped her hands. "He was Ryan's partner. They were best friends."

Valerie cocked her head. "You mean Dan Robinson?"

Jessica nodded.

"He attends the early service, doesn't he?"

"I…well…I don't know for sure." She had no idea why Valerie was so interested in Dan. Unless her attraction had shown through when she jabbered on. She balled her fists, wishing she could just force thoughts of Woolly Mammoth out of her head.

Valerie went on. "He does. Quite a few people have joined the church over the last few years, but it's kind of hard to miss a guy as big as Dan Robinson." She let out a loud laugh, and Jessica offered a halfhearted chuckle.

Had her pastor's wife listened to anything she'd said? The woman had raised four daughters. All of them grew up and loved the Lord. Married nice men. Had good jobs. A few sweet kids. Everything Jessica wanted for Emily, Maddie and Izzy. But Valerie only wanted to talk about Dan?

"You say he's been helping you a bit, huh?" she asked.

"We hadn't seen him since the funeral. Then he showed up to tell me about his concern for Emily."

Jessica lifted her eyebrows when she said her daughter's name, hoping her pastor's wife would once again focus on the topic at hand—how to deal with her daughter. Her gaze fell on the wall clock, and she gasped. The girls had been outside a full fifteen minutes. One of the children's leaders would still be with them, but Jessica didn't want to abuse the woman's time. "I've got to get Maddie and Izzy."

Valerie swatted the air. "Don't worry, Mrs. Smith won't leave them."

"I know." Normally her pastor's wife gave such good advice. After a talk, Jessica would feel refreshed and ready to continue to tackle her life as a widow and mom. Today, she felt like a fool for having said so much. She cleared her throat. "Uh, thanks for listening."

"No problem. Let Dan help you with the girls. Sounds like he'd be a great support for you."

Jessica nodded slowly. "Okay." She opened the door and took a step, but Valerie grabbed her hand.

"How long has it been since Ryan passed away? I know it's over a year...."

"Eighteen months," Jessica whispered.

"That's not very long, is it?"

"I suppose not."

"And yet, it's an eternity."

Jessica looked at Valerie, searching her face for answers about how long until life wasn't so hard. Answers Valerie couldn't give.

The older woman cupped her hand and pressed it against Jessica's cheek. "God is our strength. No doubt about that. But He sends us people to be His hands and feet. His heart."

Jessica blinked back a fresh set of tears. What was Valerie trying to say?

She wrapped her arms around Jessica and whispered, "Let Dan help you."

Chapter 5

Dan parked his car in the police garage, walked into his office and plopped onto his desk chair. He was early. Hours early. But he had to get out of the house. The weekend had been anything but restful—he had agreed to watch one of his officers' dogs, and the pup had been a handful. Dan shook his head as he remembered what Tim had said while handing over the leash, *Don't worry, Sarge. He's trained.*

After the third accident on Friday evening, Dan determined that either his officer was lying or the dog was terrified of him. Dan decided the latter since the little guy didn't eat much and stayed curled up next to the front door. Despite the messes, Dan couldn't help feeling bad for the pint-size canine when he looked at Dan with sad eyes each time a car passed but didn't stop.

He'd also wrestled with wanting to call Jessica. She'd been getting ready for a dinner and dollar-movie date with the girls when he dropped off Izzy. Saturday morning he'd debated going to the girls' soccer games. They hadn't asked him. He figured they'd forgotten, but he was still unsure how much he should see them. And if he could keep his attraction at bay.

He grabbed a weathered Bible from the bottom desk drawer and flipped to the concordance, looking for a word to describe Jessica. *Widow* jumped off the page. He chose a scripture in Isaiah. "Seek justice, encourage the oppressed. Defend the cause of the fatherless, plead the case of the widow."

The verse pounded against his chest. *Defend* and *plead.* As a police sergeant, he knew the meaning of those words all too well. He flipped through more scriptures about widows and orphans, devouring how God commanded His people to care for them.

When the phone rang, Dan jumped. He looked at the clock on the wall and gasped. Over an hour had passed. Soon the office would be filled with activity. He placed the Bible back in the drawer, then answered before the third ring. "Sergeant Dan Robinson, how may I help you?"

"Hello," the voice on the other line purred. "How's Uncle Woolly?"

"Excuse me?" Dan asked. He didn't care that irritation rang in his voice. Only the girls called him that, and this woman definitely didn't sound like one of them.

"You don't remember me?"

Dan opened the top desk drawer and pulled out a pen. "Sorry. No, I don't."

"This is Miss Stephens, Izzy's teacher. Surely you remember me now." Her voice flirted through the line.

"Uh, yeah. How did you get my number?"

She giggled. "It's a police station, Danny."

He frowned and scratched his head with the top of his

pen. "I go by Dan, and you wouldn't get my number from the phone book. I'm with an undercover unit."

"You caught me," she simpered. Dan could almost visualize her lifting her manicured hands up in surrender. "I got the number from Jessica. I had a meeting with her this morning, and I asked if I could have it."

Frustration raced through his veins. This woman had a lot of gall. "Awful early for a meeting. Everything okay with Izzy?"

"Fine. Jessica just wanted to talk about the fall festival." She paused. "You sound concerned."

He cleared his throat. "Of course. Single mom. Three kids." As Ryan's friend, he wished that were the extent of his interest. If his old partner could read his thoughts from heaven, he'd want to pummel Dan. "What can I do for you, Miss Stephens?"

"I was wondering—" her voice turned breathless "—if you'd like to come to my house for dinner."

Dan pursed his lips. He couldn't deny Miss Stephens was a beautiful woman. But definitely not his type. "Sorry, Miss Stephens. I'm busy."

"Call me Amy. How about tomorrow?"

"Busy again."

"Dan." She tsk-tsked. "Are you shrugging me off?"

He sighed, placed his hand behind his neck and rubbed. "Look, Amy. No offense, but I'm not interested."

"But you're interested in Jessica, right?"

"Amy, I think you're under the wrong impression."

"I don't think so."

Dan heard the sigh on the other end.

"Take my advice. She's waiting for you to make a move—so make it. See ya."

"But—"

The phone went dead as the office door opened and

one of the officers in Dan's unit walked in. Tim Hanks smiled as he made his way to Dan's desk. "How's it going, Sarge? Brutus musta missed us. He didn't leave our bedside all night."

Dan bit back a chuckle at the name choice for the five-pound Chihuahua. "I think he missed you."

"Jeri and I sure did appreciate you watching him for us. We had a great time celebrating our anniversary in Phoenix."

"No problem at all." The words weren't exactly true, but he would watch the little terror again if Tim needed. He was one of Dan's more efficient and effective officers. Made only good arrests. Worked well with the public. Dan would do whatever he could to show his squad he appreciated their hard work.

The phone rang again. "Sergeant Dan Robinson, how may I help you?"

One of the new field officers told him about a wino who'd caused a scene when some kids tried to get on the school bus. Dan's heart twisted when the officer relayed the man's physical description. "Thanks. Tell you what. Give me the address, and I'll come out and pick up the guy."

"No worries, Sarge. I got it."

Dan shook his head, and the weight of his shoulders seemed more than he could bear. He forced himself to his feet. "No. I'm already heading out. He's a repeat offender, and I know him. What's the address?"

He wrote down the street, then hung up the phone. After grabbing his keys off the desk, he checked to be sure he was wearing his badge.

"Want me to go with you?" asked Tim.

"Nope. I got it. Thanks, though."

Dan hurried out to the police garage. He had no desire to explain to the guys that the drunk was his dad.

* * *

Jessica slipped on her robe and ran down the stairs when the doorbell rang. Spying Dan through the peephole, she tightened the sash around her robe. Self-consciously, she ran her fingers through wet hair. No makeup. Hadn't even brushed her teeth. She groaned before opening the door and pasted a smile on her face. "Dan, what are you doing here?"

He gazed at her attire, then grinned. "I was wondering if you would join me for breakfast this morning."

"Oh…well…" She crossed her arms in front of her chest and shrugged. His blue eyes seemed brighter than usual, and she found herself wishing she could run her fingers down the length of his stubbly jaw. "I'd love to, but as you can see, I'm not sure a restaurant would welcome me."

Dan chuckled and then moved his way past her. He sat on the couch and crossed his legs. "I can wait."

Jessica turned to face the audacious man and placed her hands on her hips. "Aren't we presumptuous!" She raised her eyebrows and tried to stifle a grin. "I believe you were rejected, Mr. Robinson."

He crossed his hands behind his head and leaned back against the couch. "No, I believe you said 'I'd love to, but.' Therefore I'm going to wait." He looked at his wristwatch, back at her and smiled. "But hurry. I'm starved."

Jessica shook her head. "You're on, but I'm warning you, I'm buying the most expensive thing on the menu for your obstinacy!"

"No problem."

Jessica turned and raced up the stairs. "You'll see," she hollered to him. Feeling giddy and yet ridiculous and silly, she dressed in her favorite pale blue shirt and khaki skirt. She dabbed powder on her nose, applied mascara and a light, frosty lipstick. Grabbing the gel, she scrunched her hair into wispy waves.

Surveying herself in the full-length mirror, she sobered as she realized she cared too much that Dan found her pretty. The notion seemed wrong. She was a married woman. She *was*. Grabbing her purse, she headed down the stairs, resolved to remember Dan was merely a friend.

Once at the restaurant, Dan opened the door for her. She clutched her purse. This didn't feel like an innocent breakfast. Her sense tingled at his nearness, and the musky scent of his cologne made her stomach swirl.

"How many?" the elderly waitress asked, her full smile adding more wrinkles to her aging skin.

"Just two."

Dan seemed calm as he said the words. The older woman looked at her as if she approved of Jessica's pick for a man. With her right thumb and middle fingers, Jessica rubbed the emptiness of her wedding finger. Only a few months had passed since she put away the rings Ryan had given her. She thought she'd never wear a ring of commitment again, yet here she stood on a date with Dan.

She blinked several times. What was she thinking? Commitment? Dan simply asked her to breakfast as an encouragement. They were friends. She hadn't even seen him until recently. Hadn't thought of him much in a year. And yet now she couldn't get him out of her mind. She rubbed her palms against her upper arms.

"Everything all right?"

Dan's brow furrowed in concern, and Jessica swatted the air. "Of course."

If he could read her mind just then, he'd run out of the restaurant. She needed to get her thoughts in order. To her relief, a waitress arrived and guided them to a booth. Since they both knew what they wanted to eat, they placed their orders and the woman took the menus and headed toward the kitchen.

He folded his hands on top of the table. "That color looks good on you. Complements your eyes."

"Thanks." She focused on the utensils in her hands, unsure if she could handle praise from him. Never before had she been so aware of him. He was Ryan's partner. His best friend. For years, he and Ryan watched ball games, worked on the yard, even took care of the girls when she and Kim ran around together. Not once had she considered him as a man. Heat warmed her cheeks. Not in the ways she had thought of him lately.

"Do I make you nervous, Jessica?"

She looked into his eyes. Big mistake. Kindness, true compassion stared back at her. His bushy eyebrows intrigued her, and she liked that he kept them neat and trimmed. "It's not that."

"What's wrong, then?" Dan cupped his large hand on top of hers. Big. Strong. A hand that provided protection. One she'd witnessed offering comfort and security to her girls. A hand she found herself yearning to feel pressed against her cheek.

She turned her palm upward to his and lightly traced his hand with her fingernails. She focused on the freckle beneath the knuckle of his pointer finger and the dark hairs that trailed down his arms. He truly was a woolly mammoth. "I...like this too much."

His leg shook beneath the table. "I...um..."

"Here ya go." The waitress laid the plates between them.

Jessica snatched her hand away as if she'd touched fire. She had no idea what had come over her.

"One sampler breakfast and one order of flapjacks. Is there anything else I can get ya?" The waitress clasped her hands and smiled brightly.

"No, thank you," Dan responded.

Jessica shook her head but didn't look up. She knew her face and neck must be burning red. How she wanted an excuse to run out of the restaurant, to throw herself in bed and cover her head with a pillow as she tried to block out how she'd just caressed Dan's hand and the words she'd said to him.

She shoved a bite of pancakes into her mouth. She didn't like Dan romantically. It wasn't possible. It wasn't allowable. First, she would never again consider falling for a cop. And second, he was Dan. The girls' uncle Woolly. Ryan's partner. His best friend.

She couldn't run out of the restaurant—he'd driven her. Swallowing the large bite of food, she forced a smile, determined to pretend nothing had happened. "So, how's work?"

"Going pretty good. Been busy, but things seem to be settling down. It's an ebb-and-flow kind of thing. I'm sure you remember how it is."

Jessica picked at her food with the fork. "I remember." She put down the utensil and sighed. "Do you miss him, Dan?"

"Daily."

"Me, too."

Silence engulfed them for several long moments. He stopped eating. She couldn't blame him. Her appetite was gone, as well.

Determined to shake the tension between them, she smiled again. "So, tell me, did Miss Stephens call you?"

"Yes, she did." He narrowed his gaze and pointed at her with his fork. "Thanks to you."

She chuckled. "She's beautiful. And nice."

"Not interested."

"Seriously. You should go for her. You're what, in your

mid-thirties and you've never married. Here's this gorgeous young woman ready to snatch you up, and you say—" Jessica furrowed her brow and scrunched her nose in an attempt to mock him "—not interested."

"Let's just say she's a little too aggressive for me."

Jessica shifted in her seat as she thought of how she'd momentarily lost her mind and flirted outright with him only minutes ago.

"Besides," he continued, as the seriousness in his eyes deepened, "my heart has been set on someone else for a while now."

Her stomach churned, and jealousy crept up her spine. She didn't want Dan to have feelings for someone. Inwardly, she ranted at herself. How selfish had she become that she wouldn't want love for Dan? She had known happiness in a relationship. *Which is why I want it again.*

Oh, she was a loathsome person. She had enough to deal with as a single mother to three daughters. One of whom had struggled desperately since her father's death.

Dan cleared his throat. "I was wondering if you and the girls would let me take you to see a movie this weekend."

His offer interrupted her internal tirade, and Jessica gawked across the table at him. "What?"

"One of the guys at work said his little boy loved it." Dan shrugged. "The kid's about the same age as Maddie, so I figured…"

"That's sweet of you, but you don't need to—"

Dan reached across the table and wrapped his strong hand around hers. Tingles shot through her, and Jessica bit her bottom lip to hold back the wince. "I want to spend time with you all. I should have been there for you all along."

She shook her head. "You don't owe us anything."

"I know." He squeezed her hand. "I want to."

Jessica exhaled. What could she say? Maddie and Izzy had pestered her all week to see the movie. They loved Dan and would find a way to see him over the weekend anyway. She nodded her consent while praying God would take away her attraction to him.

Chapter 6

Jessica placed the top wheat bun on the last sub sandwich. She was done preparing the students' lunches and she could hardly wait for the school day to end. Dan had agreed to take Izzy and Maddie to soccer practice so she and Kim could take Emily shopping for makeup.

She pulled the plastic gloves off her hands and dropped them into the trash. After prayer and talking with Kim and Valerie, Jessica decided to surprise Emily for her thirteenth birthday and allow her to start wearing makeup. Kim set up a time with her cosmetologist after school for a consultation and training session. By the week's end, Jessica's oldest girl would become a teenager and start to look like one.

Her heart twisted with bittersweet anticipation. Normally she stayed in the kitchen during the eighth grade lunch wave, but today she wanted a quick glimpse of her daughter while she still looked like a young girl. Jessica peeked around the corner and scanned the massive cafeteria. It took a minute, but she finally saw Emily sitting at one of the tables farthest from the kitchen. Randy Mullins sat beside her.

When she'd first seen the boy, she felt bad for him. He was bigger than most of the other students, already had a lot of facial hair and looked closer to graduating from high school than middle. His clothes hadn't been ironed and she could see holes in his jeans.

He put his arm around Emily, and Jessica pressed her hand against the metal doorjamb as she fought the urge to bound over to them and say something. She blew out a breath when one of the principals walked by the young couple and Randy removed his arm from around Emily.

"Looking at your girl, ain't ya?" asked one of the older servers.

Jessica nodded. "I don't usually get to see her."

"Well, ya need to be opening your eyes more. That boy she's takin' a likin' to ain't nothing but trouble. Just look at him."

She fought between the urge to ask questions or to defend her parenting. "Looks can be deceiving."

"Hmph. I know that boy's mama. Bad blood's what he has. Better keep your girl away from him."

Jessica didn't respond, just stared as Emily's head rolled back as she laughed at something someone at the table had said. Jessica thought of Dan's concern that Emily would associate with Randy. Fear shifted to panic as her chest tightened. What might happen to her daughter if she didn't come out of her rebellious streak?

Jessica had to get out of there before she embarrassed Emily. Her shift had ended, so she rushed to the van and drove to the White Tanks Mountain. Despite the midday heat, she walked hard and fast through one of the trails. Her mind spun one awful scenario into another, the latter outcome always worse than the one before it. She plopped down on an oversize rock and rested her elbows on her knees. She dipped her head and begged God for guidance.

Unable to stand the heat any longer, she trekked back to the van. She cranked the radio, allowing the Christian music to drown out the fears assaulting her. Once home, she cleaned up quickly before Dan and the girls arrived at the house.

Kim barreled through the door first. "Are you ready?" She wound her arm around Jessica's. "This is going to be so much fun." She cocked her head, then tapped Jessica's nose. "Have you been working outside today? You've gotten a little sun."

Tucking her anxieties deep in her gut, Jessica forced a laugh. "Nope. Just took a little walk after work."

"Something's wrong."

Jessica shook her head. "Today is going to be a good day. Worries can wait for tomorrow."

"You checked out the college, didn't you?"

"No." Jessica smacked her hand against her thigh. "I am not you, Kim. I have no desire, no energy, to go back to school right now. I don't even know what I would want to major in."

Kim studied her until Jessica peeked out the front door. As emotional as she'd been, if Kim prodded her too much, she'd share things that could wait for another day.

"Okay," Kim finally said. "I'll stop asking, but I only want what's best for you."

"I know." Jessica hugged her sister. "And I appreciate you so much, but we have different goals."

The bus stopped in front of the house, and the girls jumped out and bounded up the walk. Izzy wrapped her arms around Kim's waist. "Aunt Kim, are we going for ice cream?"

Maddie squealed as she clapped her hands. "Really? Are we?"

Emily hugged Kim and smiled. "Hi! I'm so glad you're here."

Jessica threw her hands in the air. "I'm kinda feeling like chop suey over here. Nobody's glad to see me."

"I suppose I can be glad to see you," Dan's deep voice boomed through the door.

Jessica's heart flipped and her cheeks warmed. The younger girls shifted their attention from Kim to Dan.

"What are you doing here?" giggled Maddie.

"I'm taking you to soccer tonight."

"Me, too?" Izzy bounced beside him. "What about me?"

"Both of you." He bent down and whispered loud enough for all of them to hear him, "Get your practice clothes on and we'll get some ice cream first."

Maddie and Izzy cheered as they raced up the stairs to their rooms.

Jessica crossed her arms and feigned annoyance. "They might throw up if they eat a bunch of ice cream before practice."

Dan swatted the air. "Nah. They'll be fine. So, when are you all leaving?"

Emily frowned. "Where are we going?"

Kim straightened her shoulders and then clapped in excitement. "Well…" She glanced at Jessica and wrinkled her nose. "You agreed to it, and you're her mom, so you tell her."

A slight smile formed on Emily's lips. "Tell me what?"

Jessica rubbed her upper arms with both hands. "I've done some praying and some talking to other women. Kim. The pastor's wife."

Emily's eyebrows rose. "Yeah?"

"And I've decided to start letting you wear makeup since

you're turning thirteen this Friday. Tonight we're going to a cosmetologist who will show you what to wear and how to wear it."

Emily squealed. "Really!" She wrapped her arms around Jessica, and Jessica almost cried at the full embrace. "I'm going to change clothes and call Aleea." Happiness shone on her face and she pulled out of the hug. "When do I need to be ready?"

"Fifteen minutes," Jessica said.

"Okay." She ran up the stairs.

"She's gonna be all right." Dan touched Jessica's forearm, and again tingles shot through her veins. He winked, and she swallowed a knot in her throat.

Jessica glanced at her sister. Kim smirked and puckered her lips to tease her as she had done when they were younger and Jessica brought a boyfriend home. This time, Kim was very wrong. Dan Robinson was not, and never would be, her boyfriend.

Dan crossed his arms in front of his chest and leaned back on his heels as he looked from one field to the other. He couldn't have hoped for a better setup. Both girls had practice at the same time, at the same place, and on side-by-side fields.

When her team scrimmaged, Izzy chased the ball like a bull after a red cape. In her determination to get the ball into the goal, she ran over everyone, even the goalie. Maddie, on the other hand, was more timid. She ran to the ball when it was near her, and kicked when she was supposed to, but didn't seem quite as passionate as Izzy.

Izzy's practice ended first, and she kicked the ball as she bounced over to him. "Bet I can shoot a goal past you."

He pulled her ponytail. "You think so, huh?"

"Hey," she squeaked as she tightened the band around her hair. She nodded. "Yep. I can get past anybody."

Maddie's team was still practicing, so he chased Izzy back onto her soccer field. He bent his knees and leaned forward in front of the goal. Waving his arms up and down, he leaned left, then right. "I don't think you can do it, Izzy."

"Yes, I can." She crinkled her face and squinted. Dribbling the ball with her feet, she moved to his left, then right. She kicked, and he deflected it easily. Undeterred, she dribbled toward him again. Before he knew it, Maddie had joined the game. The two girls passed the ball back and forth, took shots, and he stopped each one of them.

Maddie kicked again, and he caught the ball and held it up in the air. He chuckled. "Give it up, girls."

Izzy ran from the sideline dribbling another ball. Before he had time to respond, she kicked it into the goal past him. Izzy squealed and ran to Maddie for a high five.

Dan scooped her up and tickled her belly. "I think that's cheating, little lady. You can't have two balls."

Maddie jumped up and down clapping. "You never said that. We beat you, Dan."

He put Izzy back on her feet, then wiped the sweat from his brow. "I think we've earned some pizza. What do you think?"

"Yeah," the girls cheered, then raced to the car.

Dan straightened his shoulders and arched his back. The girls had given him more of a workout than he'd expected. Instead of hitting the gym, he should just join them for practice. As he walked to the car, he texted Jessica to let her know he was picking up dinner. She texted back, telling him not to worry about it, but he ignored the message and called the girls' favorite pizza place.

With the pizzas in hand, he and the girls walked up the

driveway. The door jerked open, and Emily smiled. "What do you think?"

"Wow," said Izzy.

"You look so pretty." Maddie touched her sister's cheek.

Emily giggled and she batted long eyelashes. "I love it." She looked up at Dan. "What do you think?"

That she looked way too old. That he'd have to set up informants at the middle school to be sure no one messed with her. "You look beautiful, Em."

She straightened her arms and clasped her hands, twisting back and forth. "I feel really pretty."

"You were beautiful before, too."

She shrugged, blushing. "You have to say that because you're Uncle Woolly."

"No. I say it because it's true."

Kim motioned them into the house. "Emily, don't keep them outside forever. Some of us are hungry. Girls, go wash up." Izzy and Maddie raced inside and Kim grabbed the boxes out of Dan's hands. "Emily looks older, doesn't she?"

"I'll say."

Kim nodded to the living area. "Some of us don't like seeing our babies all grown up."

Dan saw Jessica standing in front of the entertainment center staring at a picture of the three girls from a few years ago. Her slumped shoulders tugged at his heartstrings. Kim and Emily had gone into the kitchen to get the table ready, and the younger girls were still upstairs. Fighting off reason, he walked to her and wrapped her in his arms.

To his surprise, she turned in his embrace and leaned her head against his chest. His heartbeat quickened. She didn't cry. She didn't speak. Dan held her, relishing the softness of her skin and the floral scent of her hair.

All too soon she moved away. He ached to touch her again but fought the urge and shoved his hands into his front pockets.

"I saw her with Randy at lunch today," she said.

Dan pursed his lips. "What happened?"

"Nothing. He put his arm around her, but when the principal walked by, Randy removed it."

"Good."

Jessica rubbed her temples. "He looks so old." She pointed to the kitchen. "Now she does, too."

"We'll keep praying, and I'll keep an eye out."

"Table's ready," Kim called from the kitchen.

Jessica nodded and then smiled up at him. "You're shirt's a little wrinkled." She pointed to his pants. "Is that a grass stain?"

"Played with the girls for a bit."

"I bet they loved that."

"So did I." He lifted his hands. "But I'd better clean up, too, before I eat any pizza."

"Yes, you'd better."

When he stared at himself in the bathroom mirror, he realized he looked a mess. Hair sticking up. Soiled shirt. Stain on his pants. And yet he'd had a blast with the girls. He washed his hands and made his way back to the kitchen.

"All I'm saying is he is one fine-looking man," Kim's voice sounded from the sink.

"I know what you're saying," said Jessica. "But you're talking like we're in high school again. There are a ton of things more important than looks."

"Of course there are," Kim said. "But it's just the two of us in here, and just because we're in our thirties doesn't mean we're blind."

Dan stopped and listened. Who were they ~~were~~ talking

about? A long sigh sounded, followed by Jessica saying, "You're right. I've always thought Dan was attractive."

He sucked in his breath.

"Dan is not attractive," said Kim. "He's an absolute hunk. Go ahead. Admit it."

He leaned forward, wanting to know how Jessica would respond.

"I admit it," she said.

Dan's heartbeat raced, and he couldn't stop the smile he felt all the way to his toes.

"He's a nine, for sure," said Kim.

Jessica chuckled. "No. He's a ten."

Jessica searched through the department store rack for a jean jacket to go with the red sundress Emily had selected. She held up a light denim one with a few weathered places. "What about this?"

Emily wrinkled her nose. "Mom, that's an awful color."

Jessica looked at the jacket Emily already held, the one she was considering. The colors seemed identical to her, but what did she know? She rolled her eyes and hung the jacket back on the rack. Next, she held up a shirt. "Didn't you say you needed a plain white T-shirt?"

"Mom, that's a scoop neck. Everyone wears V-necks."

Jessica nodded. "Right. Should have known that."

She'd just leave all selections to Emily. Simply nod and smile and agree unless Emily chose something inappropriate. Once her daughter had shopped to her heart's content, Jessica followed her to the fitting area and sat on a leather ottoman outside the room. "Just show me what you like."

"Okay."

Jessica checked her smart phone to be sure Valerie or the girls hadn't sent her a text. She looked at the picture

Valerie had taken of her and Emily before they left for the shopping spree. "I still can't believe you're thirteen."

"Finally," Emily mumbled. "I feel like I've been a pre-teen forever."

She opened the door and Jessica studied the red sundress and jean jacket. The skirt was just long enough with the hem touching the middle of her knee. The top had an adorable sweetheart neckline. "Very cute."

"Okay." She stepped back into the fitting room. "I'm going to try on the capris outfit. I can't believe I got so much money this year."

"I know." Jessica opened her purse and tapped the birthday card Emily had received in the mail. Since Ryan's death, each of the girls had received money anonymously on holidays and birthdays. The cash was nice, but sometimes she felt a twinge of concern. Someone knew a lot about her family, and she had no idea who the person was. She'd called Dan today and shared her concerns with him. He promised to check into it, but she still felt perplexed.

The door opened again, and Emily stepped out wearing a yellow-and-white shirt and khaki capris. "Cute?"

"Cute," Jessica agreed. She pursed her lips. "I can't get over how much older you look with your makeup on."

"Yeah, Randy likes…" She stopped and bit her bottom lip. "I mean…" She stepped back into the fitting room.

Jessica gripped her purse strap and prayed God would give her the right words to say. So far their trip had been pleasant, even fun, but she was still Emily's mother. She had to be the parent even when discipline wasn't easy. "Emily—"

"I'm going to try on the white shorts and blue shirt."

"Emily, we need to talk about Randy."

"Mom, I don't want to talk—"

"Doesn't matter. You are not allowed to like that boy."

Emily opened the door. "Mom, I can't help who I like."

"You're too young."

"I'm thirteen. Everyone I know has a boyfriend."

"He's not good for you."

"You don't even know him."

"Dan said—"

"Dan hasn't had anything to do with us since Dad died. All of a sudden he shows back up, and I'm supposed to listen to what he says."

"Emily."

"It's true, Mom. Randy promised me all those rumors are lies."

"Dan knows more than rumors."

Emily shook her head. "You're not going to listen to me. You're just going to believe him."

"He would never say anything to hurt you, Emily. He..." She paused. "He was your dad's best friend."

"Dad's gone, Mom. Everything's changed."

She stepped back into the fitting room and shut the door. Jessica's heart ached. She missed her husband. She missed how close she and Emily used to be. Everyone said adolescence was a challenging time for kids, but Emily had to be more difficult than most.

Jessica stood and pressed her palm against the door. "I miss your dad so much. I don't know why God allowed his death."

Emily huffed. "Why's a good question all right."

The bitterness in Emily's tone tore at Jessica's heart. "God loves you, honey. He has a plan for your life."

"Maybe I don't want God's plan," Emily whispered.

Jessica pressed a fist against her chest. How it hurt to hear the pain behind her daughter's words. She had no answers to offer. No explanations why. She was weary to the core of her being. "God has never failed us, and will never. Even now, you're going to buy clothes with money He's provided."

"I'd rather have Dad."

"Me, too, but like you said, everything has changed."

Even though Dan had sent cash to Emily for her birthday, she didn't know the anonymous card had come from him, which meant he still wanted to buy her a present. He debated for days about what to purchase. What would a dad buy for his daughter when she became a teenager?

He had finally broken down and called Kim, who had told him Emily wanted a silver necklace with her name on it. After writing down where to buy the jewelry, he had put in an order for the necklace to be made and gift-wrapped. He hoped she liked it. She needed a father figure in her life. He'd failed Jessica and her daughters for a long time, believing he could get away with helping them simply by giving money. He wouldn't make that mistake again.

Once at the house, he knocked on the door, holding the box of glazed doughnuts he had picked up at the bakery. Emily answered, her long dark hair knotted in an enormous heap on the top of her head. Dark circles had formed beneath her eyes. Without makeup, she looked like a little girl again.

She motioned into the house. "Come in at your own risk." Pointing to the doughnuts, she added, "Don't think we'll be eating many of those for breakfast."

"What's the matter?"

"Everyone in the house has a stomach bug." She pressed her palm against her chest. "Except me. I'm taking care of all of them."

Dan cringed. "You look tired."

She clasped her hands. "Well, Izzy doesn't have the best toilet aim, especially when she's been asleep. Maddie and

Mom did fine, but the whole throwing-up escapade lasted the entire night."

"Your mom is sick, too?"

"She probably has it the worst."

"Where is everyone now?"

"Asleep. And hopefully they'll stay that way. Bathrooms are clean. Everyone has fresh lemon-lime soda and crackers."

Dan studied the young lady standing before him. His chest swelled with pride that she'd done so much to help her mom and sisters. He placed his hand on her shoulder. "Sounds like you've done a good job."

Her cheek darkened at the praise. Dan held the small wrapped present out to her. "Your birthday present from me."

"Thanks." She opened the gift, and her eyes lit up. "I wanted one of these."

"I have to confess. Aunt Kim told me."

"I'm glad she did."

When she gave him a quick hug, he kissed the top of her head. "You're a precious young lady, Em. I want you to remember that."

She bit her bottom lip, and he knew she felt unsure what to say. "Why don't you go on up to bed and let me take care of everyone else for a while?"

She yawned. "I don't think I'll argue about that."

While Emily went upstairs, Dan made his way to the kitchen. He poured a glass of milk and took out one of the doughnuts, then sat down. The chair creaked beneath him, and he pinched his lips together. After swallowing his breakfast, he rounded up a few tools from the garage. As long as he was here, he might as well fix some things around the house.

For the next hour, he tightened bolts, fixed knobs, adjusted settings, cleaned filters and checked the plumbing. Once finished with the chores that wouldn't require a trip to the hardware store, he tiptoed upstairs and checked on Maddie and Izzy. Both girls slept soundly.

Then he peeked into Jessica's room. Even with a pale face, she looked beautiful cuddled against her pillow, blond hair splayed across her cheek. He probably shouldn't be watching her sleep. Even if she was sick. He argued with himself to leave, but his feet weren't listening. She must have heard him or felt his presence, because her lashes fluttered as she slowly opened her eyes. Confusion warred with her fatigued expression.

"Do you need anything, Jessica?" He took a couple of tentative steps into the room.

"What?" She licked her lips, and he rushed over to pick up the glass of soda on her nightstand. He handed it to her and she took a quick sip. "What are you doing here?"

"I came to bring Emily her present. Then I told her to take a nap, that I'd take care of you and the girls."

Jessica lifted her hand to her head and raked her fingers through her hair. Her eyelids seemed heavy, and her words were barely audible. "I don't want you to see me like this."

"You're sick. I want to help. Would you like to try some chicken noodle soup?"

She shook her head. "You can go. I'm fine."

"I'm not going anywhere." He pressed the back of his hand against her cheek. "You're kinda warm."

"Fine. Stay." She sank back onto the pillow, and Dan knew she was anything but okay.

He went back to the kitchen and found the thermometer and ibuprofen. After reading her temperature, he coaxed her to take medicine. "You're running a fever. Not a bad one, but you'll feel better if you take some pain reliever."

She mumbled some kind of argument, but Dan ignored

her and fluffed the pillows and brought her fresh soda. He touched her cheek once more. "If you need anything, I'll be in the other room. But I'll come check on you."

Her eyes closed, and she didn't move at his words. She'd fallen asleep again. He bent and brushed a quick kiss on her forehead. "I want to take care of you for the rest of my life," he whispered before standing up and tiptoeing back into the living area.

Dan kicked off his shoes and lay down on the couch. He had no intention of going anywhere until all of his girls were well. If he had his way, he wouldn't go then, either.

Chapter 7

A week had passed since he'd taken care of Jessica and the girls. And because his squad had been doing undercover work in the evenings each night, he hadn't been able to visit them. Though he'd texted Jessica, and even called a couple of times so he could hear her voice, he missed all four of them something fierce.

Dan shuffled through paperwork, filing finished reports and organizing the rest of the stack in order of importance. Scratching his jaw, he tried not to think about the hours of work sitting in that pile.

The squad's newest rookie, Marcus Adams, strolled to his desk. The guy's dreadlocks swayed beneath a navy cap. Several thick gold chains hung from his neck, and he wore baggy jeans and a dark T-shirt. Dan grinned. "I think you look the part."

Marcus flipped several dreads. "I just wish these things were mine."

"They look good on ya."

"You know it."

Dan laughed outright.

Tim walked up to them and groaned. "Are you two ready to go?"

"Marcus is definitely ready," said Dan.

"That's right, man." Marcus flipped several dreadlocks behind his shoulder, then wrapped his hand around the bulk of the chains. "I'll be raking in the drugs and finding me some ladies." He waved at Tim's attire. "Who's gonna wanna sell to you wearing a nasty old brown ball cap and zip-up shirt?"

Tim jutted out his jaw. "I look inconspicuous. Who wants to sell to a guy so flashy he's looking to attract the cops?"

Marcus pounded his chest. "I look like I've got the money to pay." He arched his back. "Besides, I'm the decoy tonight."

Tim opened his mouth, and Dan lifted his hands. "You do know that neither of you is actually buying drugs." Marcus started to talk, but Dan stopped him. "And you're both on the same team."

Marcus and Tim laughed as they knuckle-bumped. Tim smacked Dan on the back. "We're just messing around, Sarge."

"Yeah, man. Lighten up," added Marcus.

Dan shook his head as the two walked out of the police station. He attached his gun and badge to his belt, then pulled a large shirt over his head to conceal the accessories. Grabbing the keys to the undercover van, he joined the guys in the parking lot.

Tim hopped into the van with Dan while Marcus got in the drug car, a black Mustang. Marcus drove toward the agreed-upon destination—South Maple Street. Dan followed a good distance behind him. A recorder taped to

Marcus's chest served as proof for a jury. It also kept the officer from harm's way, because Dan and Tim could hear everything muttered between Marcus and the dealer.

"Okay, I see a potential dealer just ahead of me on the corner," Marcus's voice floated over the van's radio. "I'm getting out."

Dan parked a block away from Marcus and watched the younger officer get out of the Mustang and approach the man whose hoodie and baseball cap obscured his face.

"Hey, my man, what's goin' on?" Marcus's voice permeated the van. Dan watched him slap hands with the potential dealer.

"Nothin' much. Whatcha wantin'?" the guy said.

Marcus pulled off his cap and scratched the top of his head. "Just out lookin' for a good time."

"A good time, you say?" The shorter man crossed his arms and leaned against the building.

"Yeah, know where I can find one?"

The guy didn't respond. Dan knew the dealer was sizing up Marcus, trying to decide whether or not to trust him.

The man pushed away from the building and pointed down the street. "You can find your good time on the next curb."

Marcus lifted his hands and nodded. "Okay, thanks, man." He pulled his keys out of his front pocket and headed for his car.

Dan snapped his fingers and whispered to Tim, "Must have sniffed him out."

Tim snarled, "Yeah."

"Wait." The dealer's voice was rushed.

Dan peered through the windshield and watched the guy grab Marcus's arm and turn him around.

"I may be able to help you." The dealer opened his

jacket and pulled something from inside. "What kind of good time are ya lookin' for?"

"That kind." Marcus pointed to the guy's hand. "How much?"

"Twenty dollars."

Dan started the van when Marcus reached in his pocket and handed the young fellow the money. Throwing the van into gear, Dan raced over to the twosome. Tim jumped out as Marcus swung the guy around and cuffed him, pushing his face against the building. Dan hopped out. "Good job, Marcus. Does he have the money?"

"Yep."

"Do you have the drugs?" Dan asked.

"Right here in my hand." Marcus handed Dan the package.

Placing his hand on the guy's shoulder, Dan said, "Well, buddy, looks like you won't be selling anything else tonight." He twirled the shorter man around to face him. "Randy!"

"If it isn't my good friend Officer Dan," Randy mocked. "You can't do nothing to me." He nudged closer to Dan. "I'll be home in my warm bed within an hour."

Dan growled as he assisted the delinquent into the van. "At least you're off the street tonight."

Anger surged through him. Randy was right. As a minor, he'd be home in his warm, toasty bed before the night was over.

Emily's face popped into Dan's mind. She'd been difficult, but Dan knew deep down she was still a thirteen-year-old girl broken over the loss of her father. Randy was the last person she needed to hang around with. He pulled out his smart phone and texted Jessica that he needed to talk to her when his shift ended.

Jessica had told him Emily swore the rumors about

Randy weren't true, that people judged him by his family. Dan's mouth twitched. He knew all about unfair judgment by association, but in this case, Randy was telling her lies. He came from a lawbreaking family, and he'd chosen the same path. Emily needed to know the truth.

Something twisted in his heart as he thought about Randy's young age. Only fourteen. If Randy allowed God to get hold of his life, maybe he'd change his legacy. Dan thought of himself as a young teenager, remembering the youth minister who'd taken him under his wing. Dan lifted a silent prayer to God that He would send someone to be a positive influence on Randy's life.

Jessica rang the doorbell of her pastor's home. Taking a deep breath, she surveyed the newly painted door, the perfectly manicured yard. Things she'd taken for granted when Ryan was alive. She thought of Dan and how he'd fixed several odds and ends around the house last weekend when she and the girls were sick.

The door opened, and Valerie smiled and motioned her inside. "Come in, Jessica. It's great to see you."

She rubbed her upper arms. "Finally starting to cool down a bit."

Valerie nodded. "Eighties are definitely nicer than hundreds." She crooked her hand in Jessica's arm and led her into the living area. Jessica loved her pastor's home. It reminded her of a patchwork quilt. Bits of mismatched furniture, a few antique lamps, handmade and store-bought gifts and family pictures filled each room. She closed her eyes and inhaled the heavenly scent of fresh apple pie. "Mmm, it smells so good in here."

Valerie laughed and pointed to the candle burning on the coffee table. "Believe me, it's not my cooking. You'd be smellin' ashes." She gestured to the man entering the room. "Why do ya think Walter is so skinny?"

Jessica chuckled. Valerie was known church-wide for her ineptness in the kitchen. Because of her good nature, the older woman often became the brunt of many jokes. She'd just laugh and say, "God had to give me at least one flaw."

"All right, Valerie. The woman has a purpose for coming. Why don't you let her sit down and talk?" Pastor Walter patted the back of a burnt-orange wingback chair. "Have a seat, Jessica."

"I'll get us a snack," Valerie said.

While she rushed to the kitchen, Jessica sat and crossed, then uncrossed her legs. Suddenly her stomach erupted in butterflies. Twirling a strand of hair with her finger, she was no longer sure about talking with them.

"Here." Valerie returned and handed her a bakery-bought sugar cookie and a glass of sweet tea.

"Thank you." Jessica looked at the man sitting on the couch, Bible in hand. Valerie sat beside him. Both held the kindest, most sincere expressions.

"Go ahead, honey. We prayed for you right after we got your call asking to come over. We're here for you."

Valerie's soothing tone comforted Jessica's anxious heart, and for the second time in a month, she opened up about Emily and the struggles she was having with her. She told them about Randy and homework and practices, sickness and bills and household chores. When she finally finished, she exhaled a long breath and leaned back in the chair.

"Hmm." Pastor Walter opened his Bible. "Sounds like you need a little rest. Let me read a bit of scripture to you—Matthew 11:28."

Jessica gasped. "I have that verse committed to memory. I quote it all the time 'Come to Me, all you who are weary and burdened, and I will give you rest.' But I'm still exhausted, and I don't know what to do about Emily."

She rubbed her eyes, feeling tired and weak that she couldn't handle everything. Dan had called her the night before and shared in confidence that he'd arrested Randy for selling drugs. She'd lain awake all night with chest pains and shortness of breath. She'd almost called Kim several times to take her to a doctor, but she knew panic attacks all too well, so she prayed and begged God to settle down her mind.

Valerie touched her arm. "Sometimes things are easier said than done, huh?"

The older woman's understanding caressed Jessica's soul like a soothing balm. She rubbed the back of her neck. "I haven't even told you the worst of it. Ryan's partner, Dan, has been trying to help me."

"That's wonderful. Let him help you with household chores and odds and ends," said Pastor Walter.

"You and I talked about that, didn't we?" said Valerie.

Jessica looked at her, knowing her heart seemed to hang loosely at the bottom of her sleeve. Valerie smiled. *She knows. She can tell how I feel.* "The problem is—" Jessica swallowed hard and stared at her lap "—I have feelings for him." She covered her eyes with her hand at the admission she'd made aloud. "I'm so ashamed."

Soft arms wrapped around her. "There's nothing to be ashamed about," Valerie crooned in her ear. Jessica looked up and noticed Pastor Walter had left the room. "You're a young woman. Had you planned to live the rest of your life without a husband? Sure, if that's what God called you to, but maybe God isn't calling you to that."

"But Ryan. I love him. I'm betraying him."

"No, Jessica. You're not." Valerie tightened her embrace. "Dan is quite a nice Christian fellow. Am I right?"

She nodded.

"Well, then, I'd say Ryan is in heaven jumping up and down at the prospect of an honorable man taking care of his wife and daughters."

"It feels like I'm betraying him." She looked into Valerie's eyes. "I love Ryan with all my heart."

"Of course you do, and you always will. But just like you love each of your daughters, God can open up your heart to love someone else, too."

"And Emily, what about her? She's already so challenging. What will she think if she found out my feelings for her dad's best friend?"

Valerie lifted Jessica's chin. "Now listen, that girl is grieving her daddy, no doubt about that. However, it sounds like she *needs* a father figure in her life." Valerie hugged Jessica once more. "I'll be praying for you."

For the next hour, Valerie shared scriptures and encouragement. Soon they started swapping stories about crazy things their girls had done at various stages. Emily texted, and Jessica hopped up and covered her mouth. "I've been here over an hour. The girls are waiting on their dinner."

"Eating an hour later than usual never hurt anyone." Valerie walked Jessica to the door. "I'm glad you stopped by. Think about what I said about Dan."

"I will."

Jessica hopped into the van and drove to a fast-food restaurant. She might as well consider Valerie's advice, because no matter how hard she tried, she couldn't stop thinking about Dan.

Chapter 8

Monday morning, Dan entered the courtroom. He'd arrived early to be sure everything was ready for Randy's case. To his surprise, the boy had spent the night in a juvenile facility. Usually kids were released to their parents, which had been Randy's experience in the past. *A little time behind bars might do that kid some good.*

After finding a seat behind the lawyer representing the state, Dan glanced at the defendant. Though only fourteen, Randy was big enough and strong enough to look like an everyday streetside criminal. Dan couldn't wait to get the punk away from Emily.

Randy glanced at him and snarled, but his eyes didn't match the expression. He looked scared, like a deer caught by the antlers in a thicket of woods, unable to move forward or backward. Rage at the denied freedom engulfed those dark spheres, but they were frightened and uncertain, too. Pity clutched Dan's heart.

He checked out Randy's mother and grimaced. Bunny was a known crackhead and prostitute. She'd been working the streets longer than Dan had been on the police force. He looked back at the kid trapped in a grown-up's body and living in an adult world. He wondered if Randy knew who his father was. He wondered if Bunny knew. Sorrow washed over Dan. He understood all too well what it was like to have parents who didn't act as they should.

"I call Sergeant Dan Robinson to the stand." The lawyer's voice penetrated Dan's thoughts.

He stood on heavy legs and approached the witness stand. After being sworn in, he sat in the chair and studied Randy again. The kid trembled; he was genuinely worried, scared. Something inside Dan snapped. He wanted to help Randy—mentor him in some way. At the very least, he could share the good news of Christ with him.

Closing his eyes, he remembered the youth minister who'd taken him under his wing. Probably most of the congregation had thought Vic crazy for trying to help a kid who didn't stand a chance. Dan touched the badge attached to his belt. God knew better.

Again the lawyer's voice broke Dan's train of thought. He listened to each question and answered, describing the events of the previous night. When Randy's appointed lawyer cross-examined him, the man attempted to trip Dan up on a technicality, but he kept the facts straight.

The judge left the room to make a decision. Dan couldn't stop watching Randy as they awaited the verdict. *What am I supposed to do for this boy, Lord?* A verse from Isaiah jumped into his mind. "Seek justice, defend the cause of the fatherless…." Randy didn't have a father figure in his life, and obviously needed one.

What about Jessica and the girls? Dan tried to argue with the conviction that overwhelmed him. In his heart, he knew helping Randy had nothing to do with them. The boy needed guidance. Someone to look up to and gain wisdom from. He didn't know exactly what God required of him in terms of Randy, but he'd listen for the Holy Spirit's guidance.

"All rise," commanded the bailiff as Judge Cane returned to the courtroom and sat in his chair behind the desk.

The judge peered at Randy for several moments. His nostrils flared and he squinted his left eye. "Randy Mullins, this is your third time in my courtroom. I'm telling you, boy, I'm tired of seeing you here."

He pointed his finger at Randy. "This is what I'm going to do. I'm going to put you on probation for one year. If—" the judge shook his finger "—if I see you in my courtroom again, I promise it will be the last time. I *will* send you away to a boot camp you'll not soon forget. Do I make myself clear, young man?"

"Yes, sir." Randy lowered his gaze from the judge's.

Judge Cane grabbed his gavel. "You'll hear from your probation officer this week." He slammed the instrument to the desk. "Court is adjourned."

Dan's heart pounded in his chest as he hurried over to Randy and Bunny. "Randy," he said.

The twosome turned and scowled at Dan. Bunny placed her hand protectively on her son's shoulder. "You can't do nothing to my boy, so go away." She flicked long, fake fingernails at Dan.

Undeterred, Dan looked at the boy. "Randy, I was wondering if we could meet at the Y this week to play some basketball?"

Randy furrowed his brow. "I don't think so."

"Why not?"

"Why would I?"

Dan shrugged. "I'm not trying to trick you or anything. I wanna help."

Randy stared at Dan for several moments.

His confidence growing that spending time with Randy was the right thing to do, Dan grinned and nudged the kid's shoulder. "Bet you'd have fun."

Randy pursed his lips into an angry line and then his expression softened just a tad. He looked away. "I don't know. Maybe."

"Tell you what. I'll be there right after school tomorrow. If you're there, we'll play."

"Whatever." Randy rolled his eyes and walked away.

Memories washed over Dan as he watched the boy saunter out of the courtroom. Life with his own parents had been awful. Even now the stench of sour, biting beer penetrated his senses, making his stomach swirl. Compassion for the kid enveloped him. He couldn't believe his change of heart, but he genuinely hoped the boy showed up at the gym.

Jessica slowly applied her makeup. She scrunched the layers of her hair until they lay perfectly at the top of her shoulders. Selecting her favorite royal-blue short-sleeved sweater and khaki capris, she dressed with care. She sprayed on her favorite perfume and chose a light coral lipstick. Applying the color liberally, she smacked her lips for a completed effect. She looked in the full-length mirror and surveyed her reflection. She didn't look half-bad. "Actually I look pretty good." Jessica whistled at herself, then chuckled at her silliness.

The last time she saw Dan, she'd been lying in bed sicker than she'd been in years. He'd taken such good care of her and the girls, and he had invaded her every thought since then. Even more than before. After talking with Valerie and spending a long night in prayer and soul-searching, Jessica had decided to tell Dan how she felt.

Goose bumps covered her, and she shivered. The very idea terrified her. However, she wanted to confess—no, she needed to confess. "I'm too old to play games. And most of the time, too worn out!" She chuckled. "Boy, if that's not the truth!"

Grabbing her purse and keys, she headed out the door and into the van. She pulled out of the driveway, knowing that in a matter of moments, her relationship with Dan would change—for the good or bad.

"I can do this. I can do this. I can do this." Jessica stopped at the intersection and tapped the top of the steering wheel. She laughed. "I sound like the little engine that could." She lifted her left hand and pulled an imaginary train whistle. "Toot. Toot."

Honk. Honk.

Jessica jumped at the loud sound. She looked in the direction of the noise and saw a tractor-trailer in the left lane beside her. The driver tipped his hat and winked. Humiliated, Jessica lifted her eyebrows and nodded slightly in response, then turned her head and stared out the windshield. *He thought I was flirting with him.* She wanted to crawl under the seat, but she gawked at the streetlight, silently begging it to change.

She could feel the man's eyes still staring at her. *Maybe I'm delusional.* Sneaking a peek at the truck driver, the man wiggled his eyebrows and waved. Jessica gasped and stared straight ahead again. "Change, light, change."

She glanced at the clock on her dash. This had to be the longest light ever. She tapped the top of the steering wheel. Whistling, she looked at her surroundings, everywhere but the man. Noticing her doors weren't locked, she hummed nonchalantly and then hit the car lock button.

"Are you going to change, light? Or are we going to sit here all day?" she growled at the offensive mechanism. Finally the light turned green. Jessica heard the honk of the tractor-trailer as the vehicle moved forward. She dared not look at him, and she took long, slow breaths to calm her fast-beating heart. "I can do this," she mumbled again. "I can do this. I can do this."

Jessica pulled into the police station parking lot. She checked her makeup one final time. Taking a deep breath, she got out and marched in the front door. "Dan Robinson, get ready to have your socks knocked off." Jessica flipped a stray hair from the side of her face. She rapped on the cubicle wall separating the officers.

Dan turned around. "Jessica."

Pleasure washed over her at his genuine smile. "Dan, I want to talk with you."

"I need to talk to you, too."

Jessica was puzzled. He sounded serious. She surveyed him closely. Dark, heavy bags lay under his eyes. His hair was tousled, as was his shirt. She wondered how long it had been since he'd slept. Her heart sank. The all-too-familiar feeling of dread crept up her spine. *He's going to tell me something awful, I can tell.* She swallowed. "Go ahead."

For a moment, Dan scratched at his beard. He stood, led her to another room and shut the door. "Now we can have some privacy. You go first, Jessica."

Jessica looked around at bare white walls. A small table and two lone chairs sat in the middle of the room—an interrogation room. Well-known worry replaced her giddy feelings. She had no doubt he had something awful to share. "No, really, Dan. You go first."

He sat and raked his hand through his hair, around his jaw and finally through his beard. "I told you we arrested Randy a couple days ago."

"Yes. You didn't tell me why. Said you'd share more soon." Jessica sat in the chair opposite Dan. She clasped her hands on top of the table. "And…"

He frowned. "He sold drugs to one of my men. The judge placed him on probation this morning. I plan to spend some time with the boy, try to help get him on the right track."

Jessica raised her eyebrows. "You are?"

"Yeah." Dan picked invisible lint from the table. "I think you need to tell Emily to stop seeing him."

Jessica unclasped her hands, spread her arms open and shrugged. Raising her eyebrows, she smiled sarcastically. "Of course."

He frowned again. "Jessica, I'm not kidding."

"Dan, I'm not, either." She calmly clasped her hands on top of the table once more.

He straightened his shoulders. "Are you mocking me?"

Miffed, Jessica looked at her hands. *One more thing, God—just one more thing.* Slowly, she lifted her gaze to meet Dan's. Exasperated, she stood and lifted her hands into the air. "I don't know what to do. Pull her out of school? Why don't they pull Randy out?"

"Now, Jessica."

"If I tell her the sky is blue, she demands that it's green." She nodded. "We've had a few good moments lately. It's true. But that's probably because I've avoided talking about that boy altogether."

She grabbed the sides of the table and pinned Dan with her gaze. She was losing it; she could feel it. Anger, instability and defeat welled within her. There would be no more coping. She was beyond coping. Today seemed as good a day as any to be transported to the loony bin. She might very well enjoy the peace she'd find there. No, Emily would find some way to drive her crazy even from there. *Wait a minute, won't I be going there, because I* am *crazy.*

"Jessica…"

She lifted her hand to stop him from finishing. "No, Dan. I'm trying to protect Emily. I feel like she's too young for all this." She waved her hand. "This stuff this Randy kid is going through. I mean, he's just a kid, as well. What is he doing messing around with things like drugs?"

Pain pierced Dan's heart like a knife. "Some kids don't see much good in their lives."

After several moments of silence, Jessica peeked at the man sitting across from her. Weary concern covered his handsome face. Ocean-blue eyes stared at worn calloused hands. Jessica had the almost uncontrollable urge to rake her fingers through his short brown hair. She longed to feel his mustache…

Leaning across the table, Jessica trailed her fingertips across his stubbly jaw. Surprised eyes stared into hers. She lowered her gaze to his mouth. Without thought or reservation, she moved closer and claimed his lips. He kissed her back, and Jessica wrapped her hand around the back of his neck. She couldn't think. She couldn't breathe.

"Sarge, you in there?" A voice from the other side of the door halted the kiss.

Jessica pulled away from Dan in shock. She gasped and touched her mouth. "Oh, Dan, I'm…"

"Just a minute," Dan called. He stood. "It's gonna be okay, Jessica." Then he walked out.

Jessica sat stunned. Her mouth still burned from the feel of his lips pressed against hers. She'd made a fool of herself. Never again would she be able to look him in the eye. She jumped to her feet and scurried out of the building. She *would* stop thinking about him.

Chapter 9

Dan dribbled the basketball between his legs and launched a three-point shot. The ball bounced off the rim, and he caught it, shot again and made the basket.

"That cruddy shot would have cost you the game if I'd already been here."

Dan turned at the sound of Randy's voice and high-fived the kid. "You made it again."

Randy shrugged. "Ain't got nothing better to do."

"You surprised me last week."

"That I showed up?"

"No. That you could actually hit the basket…." Dan dribbled the ball past Randy and shot a lay-up. "Hit it sometimes."

Randy huffed as he scooped up the ball from beneath the basket. "I smoked you last week, Grandpa."

"Grandpa, huh?" Dan swiped the ball out of Randy's hands. The boy held up his arms to block Dan's shot. The game was on, and Dan held nothing back. Randy had a lot of pent-up frustrations, and the basketball court seemed to be a good place to release some tension.

Half an hour passed, and Dan lifted his hand. "Need a break." He panted. "Gotta get a drink."

Randy smirked as he pushed hair dripping with sweat away from his eyes. "What I tell you, Grandpa?"

Dan gulped half a water bottle, wiped his brow with the back of his hand. "Fine. I'm Grandpa."

Randy chuckled, then swallowed his drink.

Dan sat on the bench and opened his gym bag. Finding a hand towel, he wiped the sweat off his face. "So, how is school going?"

"All right, I guess."

"Staying out of trouble?"

"Suppose I don't have a choice."

Randy tried to sound cool, but Dan knew better. God had softened Dan's heart for the kid since that day in court. Every new thing he learned about Randy brought back memories of his own childhood. They didn't share the same story, but they both had parents who cared more about themselves than raising their sons. Dan put the towel back in his bag. "I've been thinking. Have you considered trying out for the basketball team?"

Randy snickered. "Pretty sure the coach don't want me on there."

"How do you know? Ever tried out?"

Randy rubbed his hands together. "Let's just say I spent a little time in in-school suspension for a prank I played."

Dan frowned. "What did you do?"

Randy wrinkled his nose. "I kinda locked the guy in the equipment room after class one day."

"Why?"

"He embarrassed me in front of everyone. Called me out for something I didn't do and made me run laps."

Dan stared at Randy until the kid finally shrugged.

"Okay. Maybe I did do it, but he still embarrassed me."

Dan shook his head. "If I talk to the coach, and he agrees to let you try out, will you?"

"I guess."

"And you'll apologize."

"But—"

"No buts. You have to respect authority." Dan locked gazes with Randy's until the kid's demeanor shifted.

"Fine. I'll apologize."

"Good." Dan punched his arm. "You got a ride home?"

Randy shook his head. "I'll walk."

"How 'bout I drive you? We can pick up a burger on the way."

While Randy chewed on the offer, Dan stood and hefted the gym bag over his shoulder. "Come on. I'm hungry."

Randy shrugged. "Fine."

"You know any words besides *fine?*"

"None you wanna hear."

Dan clicked his tongue. "Oh, so he's an overgrown smart aleck."

Randy snapped the front of his T-shirt and grinned. "Guilty as charged."

"Come on." Dan led him to the truck, got him some dinner, then drove him home. He waved when Randy hopped out of the cab and climbed up the steps to the aged apartment complex. He wondered how many nights Randy fed himself whatever he could find. Probably too many to count.

Dan tapped his phone. Tonight Randy had shared his cell number. Dan would make it a point to text him every day to check up on how things were going.

Which reminded him…he checked his messages to see if Jessica had responded to him. She'd avoided him since the day she marched into the police station and sent his head spinning with a kiss. She hadn't responded to his texts.

He grinned as an idea popped into his head. Soccer had ended. The girls didn't have any new practices starting up yet. He punched in a message that he'd be at her house in an hour to take her to dinner. He bit his bottom lip and tapped the side of the phone, unsure if he should actually send the message.

He remembered her bright blue eyes filled with sincerity and her soft, warm lips when they stayed puckered just a second too long after they'd kissed. He pushed the send button and tossed the phone on the passenger's seat. Shifting into gear, he drove back to his house for a quick shower. Once clean and dressed, he looked at his messages again. Jessica had responded with one word. *Fine.* Laughing out loud, Dan combed his hair and sprayed on some cologne. That must be the word of the day.

As excitement swelled in his chest, his thoughts shifted to Ryan. He still struggled with guilt for his feelings. Ryan wanted his family taken care of. He'd even made Dan promise, and no one would cherish them as much as Dan. But making Jessica his wife…he felt like such a backstabber, such a betrayer.

Regardless, he and Jessica had to talk. He had to know what she wanted. Maybe she could show him how to feel less guilty.

Jessica twisted her diamond stud earring as she stared at the menu. Emily had pitched a fit when she told the girls she and Dan needed to talk and would be having dinner. She accused Jessica of chasing after Dan, her dad's best friend. Closing her eyes, she again relived storming into the police station and kissing Dan on the lips. Her cheeks warmed with embarrassment. And the pleasure she'd felt.

A young brunette bounced to their table, pen and pad in hand. Her ponytail swung back and forth with each cheerful step. "How are y'all today? I'll get your drink order."

Dan smiled. "You must not be from Arizona."

She lifted her right hand. "Guilty as charged. Just moved here from Tennessee."

"For school?"

"Yeah. My grandparents live in Phoenix, so I decided to move here for college." She bobbed her head. "I like it pretty good so far. Everyone's been right nice." She tapped the pad. "So, what'll ya have to drink?"

"I'm ready to place my food order, as well." Jessica pressed her hand to her chest, then glanced at Dan. "You ready?"

"Sure."

Jessica folded the menu and slid it to the end of the table. "I'll have the nine-ounce sirloin, cooked medium-well, a baked potato with butter, sour cream and chives and a side salad with poppy seed dressing. The meal does come with rolls, right?"

Writing determinedly on the small pad, the girl nodded, but never looked up.

Dan blinked. "I'll have the same."

"Sounds good," said the waitress. "What'll y'all have to drink?"

"Coke," they responded at the same time.

"Aren't you two just as easy as pie? We'll have that out to you soon as we can."

Jessica folded her hands together on top of the table. She glanced out the window, turned to look at the people sitting across from them. Anywhere but Dan's face. He touched her hand, forcing her to look at him. She frowned at his expression of mirth. "What?"

"I thought women were supposed to eat garden salads with light dressing and nibble club crackers."

Her jaw dropped open as she crossed her arms in front of her chest. "I can't believe you just said that."

Dan laughed.

She leaned across the table and glared at him. "Are you making fun of me?"

Dan put his hands in the air in surrender. "No way."

Hackles rose on her neck. She pointed her index finger at him. "Dan Robinson, I'll have you know I missed lunch, and I would have eaten with my girls an hour ago if you hadn't texted me. I am hungry, and I am not about to eat a salad just because *you* think it's more appropriate."

Dan grabbed her index finger and hand in his. Lowering it to the table, he squeezed gently and smiled. "Honestly, Jessica. It's funny to see you order such a big meal, but it's great to see a woman actually order what she *really* wants." He shuffled his eyebrows and winked. "We both know you don't hold back."

Her face burned hot as a summer day in the desert. He was referring to that kiss. She inwardly growled. What had she been thinking? She'd wring one of her girls' necks if they threw their kisses at a boy the way she had. Covering both cheeks with her hands, she searched her mind for something to say.

"I kinda like it."

She looked into his mischievous eyes, and her heart pounded against her chest.

"Here ya go." The waitress placed their soft drinks on the table. "I'll be right back with your food."

Thankful for the diversion, Jessica popped the straw out of its wrapper and placed it in her drink. Taking a slow sip, she glanced at Dan. He winked at her, and a shiver raced down her spine. Emily had been right. Her mom had fallen for her dad's best friend. But how should she deal with that?

After the waitress returned with their food, Dan dug in and shoved a huge piece of A.1.–dripping meat into his mouth. He sipped his drink, then wiped his face. The sequence was one she'd watched Ryan do a million times. It made sense he and Dan would share some nuances. They'd spent as much time together as she and Ryan had. That was probably why she'd fallen in love with him.

Jessica patted her mouth with a napkin. "Tell me about yourself."

He raised one eyebrow. "Gonna ignore the elephant in the room?"

Jessica grinned and nodded. "Yep."

"Okay by me." He wiped his hands on the napkin. "What do you want to know?"

Jessica bit into her roll. "Do you have any sisters or brothers?"

"Nope."

"What about your parents?"

"My mom's dead."

"I'm sorry." She jabbed at her baked potato. "My mom passed away when Kim and I were just kids. We lived in Ohio at the time. It had snowed, and Mom was coming home from work. Hit an icy patch." She pursed her lips. It had been a long time since she'd talked about her mother.

"It was hard, I'm sure."

She laid down her fork and placed her elbows on the table and leaned forward. "You know, I barely knew her. I was only five, and I just have snapshots of memories."

"I didn't know you lived in Ohio."

"We moved that year. Dad said he didn't ever want to

see another snowflake as long as he lived." She picked up her roll and broke it in two. "How did your mother pass away?"

"Drug overdose."

She sat back in her seat. "Wow. I'm so sorry."

Dan rubbed his chin. "I guess that's why I feel like I need to help Randy. His mom's a mess. Dad's not around." He flipped his wrist. "I've been there. Know what it's like."

Jessica blinked several times. "You don't know your dad?"

Dan frowned and nodded at the same time. "No. I know him. He lives at the Renewed Hope Center half the time." He shifted in his seat, looked out the window, then back at her. "You have to be sober to stay at the center. Since he's drunk so frequently, he spends half his time on the streets and the other half there."

Jessica sucked in a breath and covered her chest with her hand. "He lives here?"

"Yep. I used to try to help him, but he wouldn't hear of it. Hates that I'm a cop."

Jessica didn't know what to say. She'd never known that Dan had had a hard life growing up. Despite having only her dad and sister, she'd had a good life. Ryan had, as well. Even if she hadn't heard much from his parents since Ryan passed, she knew his growing up years were good.

"What about your dad?" asked Dan.

"Died from cancer the year after Ryan and I married."

Dan nodded. "I'm sorry."

Jessica twirled the paper napkin between her fingers. Such a morbid topic she'd chosen for them, and yet she wanted to know more about his dad. "What's your dad's name?"

"What?"

"Your dad's name? I'd like to pray for him."

Dan frowned and then let out a long breath. "His name's Frank."

"So, how are the two of you doing?" asked the young waitress. "You ready for some dessert?"

Dad patted his stomach. "I'm stuffed."

Jessica wanted to lighten the mood. Eventually they'd need to talk about what was going on between them, or at least what they wanted from each other, but for now she wanted to see him smile again. She eyed the pamphlet of desserts at the end of the table. "I think we should split the chocolate mousse pie."

Dan's jaw dropped. "Are you kidding?"

She swatted his hand. "Dan, you better stop acting surprised that I actually eat every now and then."

The brunette chuckled and leaned toward her. "Miss, you look good. Don't let your old man tease you into believing otherwise."

Her face warmed at the thought of him being her husband, but she laughed anyway. "Go ahead and bring one to us."

When the girl walked away, Dan captured her gaze with his. "We still haven't talked about the reason you're avoiding me."

Thankful the waitress hadn't taken her napkin, Jessica twisted it with both hands. "I think you know why."

"Yes, and I want—"

"Emily was furious I was coming to dinner with you. She thinks I'm chasing after her dad's best friend."

A pained expression swept across his face, and he clasped his hands. She wished she could bite her tongue. Why had she just blurted that out? A sane man would run for cover from her and her three daughters. Moody and miserable most days, they were a difficult group for Ryan at times, and he'd helped create three of them.

"Jessica, I think you're a beautiful woman, but—"

But? But. The infamous *but.* Jessica didn't want to hear more. She really didn't think she could handle it. She was a fool for falling in love with Dan in the first place, but she'd gone and done it. Couldn't take it back. She lifted her hand to stop him. "Listen, Dan. I don't know what came over me. I'm exhausted most of the time, and I guess at that moment I just needed..." She scrunched her nose. "I don't know what I needed, but I shouldn't have done it. I'm sorry."

"You don't have to be sorry."

"Yes. Yes, I do. It was ridiculous of me." She pointed to him, then back at herself. "I mean, you and me." She laughed. "What a crazy idea."

Dan frowned and opened his mouth, but the waitress showed up with the dessert. Jessica tapped the side of the plate. Touched her stomach. "You know what? I'm actually not feeling so good." She looked from Dan, then back at the waitress. "Will you box it up so I can take it home?"

"Sure thing," the girl cooed. She placed the bill in front of Dan. "You get her home and take care of her."

Now she really did feel sick. Jessica swallowed back a wave of nausea. "I'm gonna have to meet you in the car."

Chapter 10

Jessica hadn't heard from Dan since their dinner date, and she couldn't stop thinking about his father. An idea formed, and she bit back a chuckle as she walked into the kitchen. Emily, Maddie and Izzy sat at the table eating breakfast. "Girls."

Three heads bobbed her way in unison. She hoped they would be as excited as she was. "I have an idea for a family ministry."

The younger girls' eyes glazed with merriment. Emily rolled hers, then stared at the table.

"What is it?" asked Izzy.

Glancing at Emily, Jessica determined not to let her oldest child spoil this idea. She looked at the excited anticipation on the faces of Izzy and Maddie and smiled. "Well, Uncle Woolly told me his dad sometimes spends the night at the Renewed Hope Center. I believe they let people volunteer to help in the kitchen. Maybe they'd let us. What do you think?"

"What's the Reviewed Hope Center?" asked Izzy.

"Renewed," Jessica said, "it's a house for people who don't have a place to call home."

"Dan's dad doesn't have a place to live?" asked Izzy.

"Why doesn't he stay with Dan?" said Maddie.

"What? Is he a drunk or something?" Emily retorted.

Jessica sent a warning glare at her oldest. "I will take your phone away from you for a month."

Emily huffed and pursed her lips together.

"I don't know all the answers to your questions," Jessica continued. "Dan just told me that his father stays there sometimes."

"Did he tell you that when you went on your date?" piped Izzy.

Emily smirked.

Jessica blinked. "It was not a date. It was just dinner."

Maddie clapped. "I think it sounds fun."

"Can I wash dishes there?" Izzy jumped from her chair and grabbed Jessica's arm.

"Oh, to be five again and actually *want* to do the dishes." She patted her daughter's head. "If they'll let you, I don't mind if you help with dishes."

"Yippee!" Izzy yelled.

"When can we go, Mom?" Maddie asked.

"Well…" Jessica kissed the top of Izzy's head. "Since you're out of school on fall break, I thought we'd go today."

"Hooray!" Maddie and Izzy hollered.

Izzy lifted her finger. "Did you know Steven Spielberg used to live in Arizona? Miss Stephens said he's the man who made the alien movie."

"What alien movie?" asked Maddie.

"The one Mom liked when she was a kid," said Izzy.

Maddie scratched the top of her head. "I don't know

which one Mom liked." She shook her head. "I don't like alien movies."

"She's talking about *E.T.*" Jessica smiled, trying to appreciate Izzy's new pleasure of sharing all of Miss Stephens's fun Arizona facts.

Maddie snapped her fingers. "The one where the alien phones home."

Izzy stuck her finger up in the air and lowered her voice. "E.T. phone home."

Emily shifted her weight from one foot to the other. "Do we have to go today?"

"Yes." Jessica placed her hand in the small of her oldest daughter's back. "Let's try to have a positive attitude about this."

"I get to sit by the window on Mom's side," said Izzy.

"No fair," whined Maddie.

Jessica groaned. "Why must we always argue about where to sit in the van? I have half a mind—"

"I'm staying home," Emily interrupted.

Jessica smiled, determined not to get angry. "No, you're going." She clapped her hands. "Everyone, go make your beds. We're leaving in half an hour."

Two smiling faces and one sulking one accompanied Jessica as she pulled into the parking lot of the Renewed Hope Center. The facility was run from an old two-story home. Brown rock wrapped around the bottom floor, while clean tan stucco made up the second floor. A bright yellow, orange and red wreath hung on the green door. The yard was well maintained with a large welcome sign in the front. Jessica knocked on the door, and someone hollered, "Come in. Door's always open."

They walked inside and a mixture of lemon cleaner and honeysuckle wafted into Jessica's nose. Polished hardwood floors and antique furniture in an array of blues and greens adorned the front room. She could see part of the dining room, and it was painted a burnt orange, accented with yellows. The house was nice. Spectacular. She couldn't believe it was actually a shelter.

"Good afternoon," a short, red-haired woman greeted them. She grabbed Jessica's hand and shook it. "Can I help you?"

Jessica read kindness and compassion in the woman's eyes, but there was feistiness, as well. Plus, she packed quite a strong grip. This woman might be tiny, but Jessica believed she'd take on anyone who dared go against her. "This is the Renewed Hope Center, isn't it?"

Concern etched the woman's brow. Her gaze quickly took in each of them. "Yes. Are you needing help? Most of my guests are men." She winked at the girls. "Grumpy at that. But I couldn't stand to turn anyone away."

Jessica pressed her palm against her chest and patted Maddie's shoulder. "No. We'd like to help *you!*"

The woman's brow furrowed into confused lines.

Jessica continued. "The girls are out of school for break. We wanted to help you as a ministry. That is, if you need any help."

The woman smiled so fully her eyes seemed to disappear. "Of course I have things you can do. I'd never turn down people wanting to help others." She gathered all four of them toward her, then led them to the kitchen. "My name is Betsy Nichols." She kneeled in front of Maddie and Izzy. "Can you girls wash dishes?"

Izzy's eyes lit in delight. "Yes, ma'am."

Maddie's eyebrows rose and she nodded dramatically.

"Well, then." Betsy cupped Maddie's chin. "Why don't you wash?" Then she poked Izzy's stomach. "And you dry."

"All right!" the younger girls answered in unison.

Betsy led them to the sink and filled it with bubbly lemon-scented soapy water. Handing Maddie a washcloth and Izzy a hand towel, she turned the twosome loose on a sink full of plastic plates and glasses. Perfect for beginners.

The older woman looked at Emily, whose face expressed pure disdain. "Hmm." Betsy placed a finger to her mouth and twitched her lip to the side. Jessica wondered if the woman could tell Emily had to be forced to come.

Betsy wrapped her arm around Emily's shoulder. "I believe I have just the job for you." She started to lead Emily out of the room, then stopped. Turning back to Jessica, Betsy pointed at the far wall and said, "Just set the tables in the dining room for me, please. The plates and silverware are in that cupboard."

"Sure." Jessica retrieved several plates and napkins, then walked into the dining room.

She gasped at the elegant setting. A long mahogany table seating at least sixteen people sat in the middle of the room. An antique crystal chandelier hung from the ceiling above the middle of the table, which was covered with a clean white tablecloth. Spanish artwork burst with bright yellows, oranges and reds on the walls. Jessica laid the plates and napkins in front of each chair and wondered about the shelter Betsy had opened. This place looked more like an expensive bed-and-breakfast.

Soon a group of surly looking men flooded the room. Each appeared clean, though probably not most of the time. Stringy hair and rotting teeth could not be fixed with mere soap and water.

A tall, thin man walked in and sat at the chair on the far left end of the table. Jessica studied him. Shoulder-length tangled hair and dingy, too-small clothes almost hid his identity, but penetrating blue eyes gave him away. He must be Dan's dad.

A longing to help and protect welled in Jessica. She wanted to wrap her arms around the man and tell him life had more to offer him than a shelter. God had more to offer him. Of their own accord, her feet moved toward the man. She stopped just out of reach.

A sour, biting odor burned her nostrils. It wasn't the smell of fresh alcohol, but of stale dried-up bourbon. Jessica's stomach lurched.

He looked at her and grinned. Yellow teeth appeared. He winked. "Can I help you, little lady?"

"No," she squeaked, and ran for the kitchen. Leaning against the cupboard, she grabbed a napkin and wiped the sweat forming in small beads on her forehead. She grabbed a cup from the pile of dishes beside Izzy. "Excuse me, Izzy." Jessica moved the spigot away from the soapy water and turned on the cold. After filling the cup, she took a slow drink and wiped her brow again.

"You okay, Mom?" Maddie touched Jessica's hand.

"Yeah, you don't look so good," said Izzy.

Jessica put the cup in Maddie's soapy water and smiled at her daughters. "I'm okay. How are you two doing?"

"Great." Maddie stuck both hands deep into the water and rubbed the washcloth against a dish. "This is fun. Can we do this again?"

Jessica twisted her diamond stud earring. "Uh, sure."

Betsy walked into the kitchen without Emily. Jessica wondered what the woman had her oldest child doing. She worried Emily had given her a hard time about whatever it was. However, Betsy didn't seem upset. The woman hummed a merry tune and pulled a dish from the oven.

Panic overwhelmed her. What if Betsy asked her to serve those men? What would she say to Dan's dad? Jessica wiped her perspiring forehead with the napkin once again. She'd prayed for the man continuously since finding out he existed, and then the moment she saw him she freaked out.

Emily walked into the room, grabbed two pot holders and took the casserole dish from Betsy's grasp. With her shoulders back and head up, she made her way into the dining area. Jessica followed, fearing what Emily might say if she recognized Dan's father.

Leaning against the door, she watched as Emily placed the dish in the center of the table. Several of the men lifted their noses and sniffed the delicious scent of homemade chicken potpies. With obvious confidence, Emily looked from one man to the next. She stopped on the man who looked so much like Dan. Emily placed the pot holders in one hand and rested both hands on her hips. "You must be Dan Robinson's dad."

Jessica gasped.

The man's eyes formed two straight slits that matched the angry, wrinkled line of his mouth. He hit the top of the table with his fist. "Who are you?"

Jessica swallowed a knot in her throat as she pressed her hand against her racing heartbeat. Emily seemed unmoved by his display. "Look, bud, I don't want to be here any more than you want me here. My mom made me come. She's the one messing with your son."

Jessica bit back a growl as she crossed her arms in front of her chest. "I'm not *messing* with anyone," she mumbled under her breath. She could not believe how crude her own child, flesh of her flesh, had become.

"Who are you?" the man asked again.

"Emily Michaels."

A glimmer of light flicked in the man's eyes. He smiled slightly. "You're Ryan's girl? Danny's sweet on Jessica?"

Jessica fell against the wall when the man said her

name. Had Frank known Ryan? Ryan had never mentioned Dan's father.

Frank slapped his leg with one hand. "Well, whaddaya know?"

Emily didn't budge. "So you *are* Dan's dad?"

The man extended his hand to Emily and grinned, exposing the rotten yellow teeth. "Frank Robinson's the name."

Emily uncrossed her arms and balled her fists at her sides. Stomping the floor, she spit, "I don't want to be your friend!" Her eyes traveled the length of the man. "Look at you. You need to get your act together and help me with my mom and your son."

"Want them together, do you?"

Emily scrunched up her face. "No. I don't. He's like my uncle."

"Which I'd suppose makes the match perfect." Frank chuckled and swiped his hand through his hair. "But I don't talk to the boy anymore. Won't be of any help to you."

Emily stomped her feet once more. "Fine."

Jessica ducked back into the kitchen and studied Izzy's dish-drying abilities. She prayed Emily had not seen her in the doorway.

The girl whooshed by Jessica and headed up the stairs. Jessica could hear the men's guffaws at the table. Frank's voice sounded. "Feisty one, ain't she?"

He had no idea.

Dan shuffled through the paperwork cluttering his desk. He'd tried not to think about Jessica the past few weeks. She'd made it clear at the restaurant she wasn't interested. He was haunted by her words and expression when she had said a relationship between them was a crazy idea.

Picking up a pile of folders, he tried to concentrate.

"Jones. Travers. Mitchell." He flipped through each. "Williams. Mullins." He stopped.

Randy's file. Pulling it from the stack, he laid the other folders on the corner of the desk and opened the teenager's file. Randy's biographical information stared back at him. His place of residence—the worst in town. His mother—one of the city's confirmed prostitutes. His father—unknown. His age—a minor, only fourteen.

Dan snarled. The kid was nothing more than a product of his environment. What motives did Randy have to be good, to do good?

He thought of his own parents. The pain, humiliation and sadness he'd felt at various times in his young life. He and Randy had played basketball at the YMCA several times since the hearing. Each time, Dan asked if he'd signed up for basketball tryouts. Each time Randy said he'd get around to it.

After grabbing his keys out of his desk drawer, Dan headed to the parking garage, saying his promise aloud, "That's it. I'm going to the school right now to be sure that boy has signed up."

A smile tugged at the corners of Dan's mouth when he remembered the prank Randy had played on the coach earlier in the year. "Though I might need to make sure the coach will let him."

Dan parked in front of the middle school and then went inside and signed in at the front desk as a visitor. He made his way to the gym and read the tryout sheet posted on the door. Randy's name wasn't on the list. After penciling in the boy's name, Dan pushed open the door to the small office on the right.

"When do tryouts start?" he asked the coach.

The stout, balding man scratched the back of his head. He crossed his arms and leaned against the desk. Metal screeched against the concrete floor as the man's weight proved too much for the office furniture. "Next week. They're open to anybody who isn't on academic probation and who's passed a physical."

The stench of body odor penetrated Dan's nostrils. He felt claustrophobic standing mere inches from the middle school coach in this small office. Dizziness swept through him. He wondered if the room had once been used to store sports equipment. It surely wasn't big enough to fit two full-grown men and a desk. Closed spaces had always been a menace to him, even on the job.

He shoved his hands deep into his pant pockets and swallowed the bile in his throat. How did Coach Aspen stand working in here every day? "I've been working with a young man I'm encouraging to try out. He's a great ballplayer."

The man squinted one eye and puckered his lips. "Who are you talking about?"

"Randy Mullins."

Coach Aspen released a loud sigh. He got up and edged his way closer to Dan. "Look," he whispered, "we both know who the boy's mom is. I don't think we need that kind of influence on the middle school team."

Dan bit back his initial retort and focused on the opportunities playing ball would afford Randy. Keep him off the streets, in practice and at games. He'd learn teamwork, how to trust his fellow players. He'd have an out from his environment, at least for a season. "His mother should have nothing to do with it."

Coach Aspen leaned back against his desk and cocked his head. "Hasn't he been caught dealing drugs?"

"Yes."

The man raised both hands in the air. "I can't have a drug dealer on my team."

"He's quit."

"He's quit," Coach Aspen mimicked. He shook his head and looked at the ceiling. "You of all people should know they've *all* quit."

The truth in the coach's statement punched Dan in the gut. Maybe Randy was trying to play him for a fool— getting on his good side so he could deal on the sly and feel confident Dan would back him up. He'd been blindsided before. By his own father. Randy could be just the same.

No, God took a chance on me. I didn't deserve it. He loved me despite my past, my upbringing and my reputation. Randy needs that chance, too.

Dan crossed his arms and stiffened his back. "He's clean. I'll get a drug test to prove it. Then I'll personally vouch for him to stay that way. I'll make sure he does."

Confusion contorted the coach's face. "Why? Why the interest in Randy Mullins?"

"Because he's just a kid in need of some guidance." Dan extended his hand. "Can he try out?"

Coach Aspen released an exaggerated sigh, then grabbed his hand and shook it. "All right. Make sure his grades are good, and he'll need proof he passed a physical. Tell him to be here on Monday after school."

"Thanks." Dan opened the office door.

"I want that drug test in my hand before he tries out. My guess is there will be a few parents asking me questions."

"You got it."

After checking Randy's grades, Dan called a pediatrician he'd met on a case and set up an appointment. The reception seemed a little surprised when he requested a drug test be completed at the same time. He called Randy. "You never told me you're a straight-A student."

"Yeah. So?"

"So I signed you up for basketball."

"Great," he replied. "Surprised Coach let you."

"He did. And I'm picking you up for a physical."

"Now?"

"Yep. Get your shoes on. I'll buy you a burger afterward."

Chapter 11

"Here, Betsy. Let me help." Jessica picked up two pot holders and took the corn-bread casserole from the older woman's grasp. It wasn't heavy, but the weight obviously gave Betsy's arthritic hands a difficult time.

Betsy wiped her hands on the apron, then stirred the soup-filled pot. "Thanks, hon." She looked at Kim. "I'm glad you came with your sister and the girls today."

Kim placed the folded dishcloths in the drawer. "This isn't the way I usually spend my Saturday morning, but I have to admit I've enjoyed myself." She pulled Izzy's ponytail. "I didn't have a choice anyway. Izzy and Maddie pestered me all week to come with them."

Izzy giggled and pried a stray hair out of her mouth with soapy fingers. Bubbles trailed her cheek and jaw. Maddie giggled as well when she tried to help her sister, but only added more soap to Izzy's face. Kim picked up a towel and wiped her face.

"Sometimes change is good." As soon as the words slipped from Jessica's lips, she thought of Dan. He'd stopped by a few times to see the girls. Emily avoided him, but he'd taken Maddie and Izzy for ice cream. Jessica didn't know what to say to him. She still thought of him constantly, even dreamed about him, but she felt like such a cheater, especially when Emily's accusations flashed through her mind.

Kim stared at her. "My thoughts exactly."

Jessica knew what she was referring to. Kim had asked her point-blank what Jessica's feelings were for Dan. Sister intuition, Kim had called it. At the moment, Jessica had been too tired to deny anything. She told her she'd fallen for him, but a relationship was impossible. He was Ryan's best friend. And he was a cop. She lifted her gaze to the ceiling. A cop! Of all the occupations, why did she have to fall for another man who put his life in jeopardy each day he went to work?

Ignoring her sister and her own frustrating feelings, Jessica smelled the savory soup, and her stomach rumbled. "What is this? It smells perfectly delicious."

"White chili."

"Do we get some, too?" asked Kim.

Betsy laughed. "Why, of course." She pointed to the pot. "Jessica, will you take this to the men? I've got another pot in the refrigerator. Just needs to be warmed up."

"Absolutely." With pot holders in hand, she hefted the soup and walked into the dining room.

"So, ya say your mama and my Danny are an item, huh?"

Jessica stopped. She couldn't move. She couldn't breathe. Emily sat beside Frank at the table. Her expression stabbed hatred into the tablecloth. Frank seemed tickled by their conversation.

"Yes, I'd say they're an item, but they won't fess up to it." Emily pounded the top of the table with the side of her closed fist. She never took her eyes from the white, linen-covered table. "They probably haven't even admitted it to each other."

Jessica swallowed. She'd gone to dinner with Dan one time, and her daughter thought she and Dan were dating? She twisted her mouth. Okay, they'd eaten breakfast together, too, but Emily didn't know about that. The teenager had gone from trying to sneak clothes and makeup and liking a bad boy to focusing her fury on an imagined relationship between Jessica and Dan.

Frank placed his index finger under Emily's chin and lifted her gaze to his. "Aw, now, honey. I don't see how it'd be all that bad for Danny and your mama to get together. Danny loved your daddy more than anyone in the world. He'd be awful good to you."

"My thoughts exactly."

Jessica jumped at Kim's whispered words from behind her. She turned and narrowed her gaze at her sister.

"I'm just agreeing with the guy." She winked and flounced back into the kitchen.

Jessica gripped the pot tighter. Her heart pounded against her chest. She stepped into the dining area, and everyone looked at her—everyone except Emily and Frank.

Her daughter glared at Frank. "Dan was no friend to my father. If he had been, he'd have never let him get shot."

Emily pushed away from the table and bolted up the stairs.

"So that's why she's so angry with Dan," Jessica mumbled.

She placed the pot of soup on the table. Her mind raced through every conversation she could remember with Emily after Ryan was shot. Had the girl ever mentioned her feelings toward Dan, or had they just surfaced? A rough, calloused hand wrapped around Jessica's. Startled, she gawked at its owner.

"Dan would be good to you girls." Frank's soft voice was a complete contradiction to the feel of his skin.

Jessica thought of all the things Dan had done for them in the past few months. He had been aloof at times but was always there when she needed him. The truth was she wanted him to be more than a friend. She knew she did. "You're right."

Frank smiled, then dipped a spoonful of soup into his bowl.

A ridiculous idea came to her mind. More than likely, she'd regret it a hundred times over, but something inside her stirred her to ask. "Frank?"

"Hmm?"

"What are your plans for Thanksgiving?"

Dan sat in the farthest corner of the bleachers. Coach Aspen had agreed he could watch the tryouts. Randy knew he was there for moral support, but he still didn't want to make his presence obvious. Dan counted heads. Twenty-two boys. Most of them stood together in small groups. Randy and a couple of other kids stood alone. Dan lifted up a quick prayer that the teenager would find someone to connect with.

Coach Aspen sniffed and hefted his gym pants higher. "All right, guys. Let's get started."

The kids gathered around the coach, and Randy glanced at Dan. Concern etched his brow, and Dan nodded to him for encouragement. The kid's mouth turned up just a bit on one side. He looked back at the coach.

He needed to see me here. God, help me be a witness to Randy just as Vic was to me.

A boy about the same size as Randy strolled from the locker room and positioned himself inches from Randy. Randy moved a few steps over. The kid did the same. Randy frowned and jutted his jaw in silent challenge. The boy puffed out his chest. Dan had just jumped from his seat to stop the inevitable fight when Coach Aspen blew his whistle. The boys looked away from each other, and Dan sat back down. He clasped his hands and rubbed his thumbs together.

"Okay," said the coach. "We're going to start with some warm-up exercises. I want to see how fast and coordinated you are. Hit the outside line."

The boys scurried to find a position. Pride swelled within Dan when Randy took the initiative and moved himself away from the boy who had bothered him.

"When I whistle," ordered Coach Aspen, "I want you to race to half court, tap the line with your hand, then race back and tap the outside line in the same manner. You will not stop until I blow the whistle again."

Coach Aspen lifted his hand. The boys crouched to a track start position with their fingers on the line, one leg bent under their body and one stretched out behind them.

The whistle blew.

The boys raced back and forth from half court to out-of-bounds and then back again. Within moments, Randy and several of the other kids proved their endurance as they kept up the pace while others grew weary and grabbed their sides. Coach blew his whistle to stop.

Dan's heart just about burst with pride. Randy grinned and high-fived a couple of the other boys. His own father couldn't have mimicked the emotion Dan felt. God had called him to this very place on this day. He'd listened to the Spirit's nudging to help this boy, and he was getting to see a good thing happen for a young man who needed it.

The kid who'd tried to start a fight moved closer to Randy, raised his elbow and jabbed it into Randy's side. Randy grabbed his midsection and glared at the guy. The boy winked and walked away.

The whistle blew again.

The boys gathered around the coach. Randy stood with his shoulders back, but he kept a hand on his side. Coach Aspen broke them up into pairs. Dan's pulse raced when he saw Randy had been paired with the bully. The contemptuous look in the boy's eyes bothered Dan. The kid was overly aggressive in dribble passes and layups. Coach Aspen had to notice the kid wasn't playing fair, but he didn't say anything.

"He can see what's going on." The words fumed beneath clenched teeth. "Whatever happened to good sportsmanship?" Dan was doing all he could to stay on the bleachers and not pulverize the lot of them. Randy needed a distraction from his life. Basketball was perfect, if they'd give him a chance.

The kid stuck out his foot. Randy toppled over it and smashed his face against the floor. Dan clenched his fists. That was the last straw. He stood.

Randy got up and dusted his shirt. A small bead of blood dotted his bottom lip. He licked the evidence away. "I'm okay."

Dan wondered if the boy had said the words to keep him from barreling to the floor and making a scene. The words were enough to calm Dan's anger. If Randy could be the bigger man, then Dan could, too.

He sat back on the bleachers and gripped the seat. Half an hour later, tryouts ended. Dan wiped the sweat from his brow. He'd had every bit as much of a workout as the kids.

Randy picked up his duffel bag and water bottle and meandered toward Dan. "So, how'd I do?"

He patted the boy's shoulder. "You did great."

"You think I have a shot at making it?" Randy popped his water bottle open and guzzled the liquid. He sat on the bleacher and fumbled for something in his bag.

Dan lowered himself beside the kid. "That coach would be a fool not to pick you for the team."

Randy looked up. Dan could see the boy sought sincerity in Dan's words. The corners of his mouth turned up. His eyes shone with pure delight. "Thanks."

Dan stared at the kid who'd picked on Randy through tryouts. He stood by Coach Aspen, the two deep in conversation. Dan hoped the coach reprimanded the boy for trying to hurt Randy. Randy lived in a bad environment, and he'd made several bad choices, but he needed a chance to change his life.

"You handled that kid better than I would have," Dan whispered.

"What?"

Dan looked at Randy. "The boy who was trying to rile you up. I want to be a Christian influence on you, but I think I would have decked him." Dan cringed, wishing he hadn't been quite so honest.

Randy grinned. "He was doing it on purpose."

"How would you know that?"

"He told me after. Coach wanted to be sure I could handle my anger." He shrugged. "Can't say I blame him. I was mad when I locked him in the equipment room." He dipped his chin. "And I might be known for having gotten into a fight or two in the last couple of years."

Dan nodded. The teenager was definitely more mature than him. And more Christ-like. Dan had planned to give the coach a piece of his mind as soon as tryouts ended. He exhaled, but if Randy understood the coach's motives, Dan would, too.

Time seemed to poke by as they waited for the coach to announce who'd made the team. He'd promised to let the boys know today, since they'd need to dress out for practice the following day. He glanced at Randy. The kid stared into nowhere. Didn't move. Didn't even look as if he was breathing.

"Okay, boys, I've made my decisions." The coach held a piece of paper in his hands. "I'm posting the team on the gym door and then I'll go to my office. If you have any questions, that's where I'll be."

Everyone watched as the man taped the paper to the door. He nodded to them all, then walked back to the office and shut the door. The boys raced to the list, but Randy didn't move. Whoops and hollers commenced, as well as slumped shoulders and frowns.

Randy glanced at him. "We'll wait till they clear out a bit."

Dan nodded, and then slugged his shoulder. "I'm rooting for you."

"I know."

Once the majority of the boys had gathered their bags and left the gym, Randy stood. Dan followed him to the gym door. They skimmed through the list until they found his name. Randy looked up at Dan and grinned. Dan clapped him on the back.

The kid who'd pushed him around sidled over to Randy. He lifted his fist. "Congratulations, man."

Randy bumped knuckles with him. "You, too. See you tomorrow."

Chapter 12

"Mom, Ms. Valerie is on the phone."

Izzy's voice carried from the other side of the house. Jessica hopped over a pile of Barbie dolls and accessories. Her heel caught the edge of Barbie's convertible. She bit her lip to conceal the yelp, and trudged past a pool of nail polishes, files and stickers.

A stray hair fell from her short ponytail and smacked her in the eye. She pushed it behind her ear and accepted the phone from her daughter. "Hey, Valerie."

In a glance, she surveyed the mess of her house. She'd worked each day this week. Emily had needed help with two projects; plus, she'd had an after-school youth outing. Maddie had started horse riding, and Izzy dance. None of them had time to keep up with the chores.

"Hello, dear. How are you?"

Jessica smiled at the sound of her friend's voice. She leaned against the dining room table. "Honestly, Valerie, I'm living in a disaster zone over here."

"Perfect."

Jessica flopped into a chair, rested her elbow on the table and plopped her chin into her hand. "You're glad my house is a mess?"

"Not at all. I just wanted to treat the girls to dinner and a movie. Give you time to get your house in order before Thanksgiving."

Jessica grinned. "And how would you have known my house is a disaster? Are you somehow spying on me?"

Valerie clicked her tongue. "I had four girls, remember? My house was always in disarray."

Scanning the toy war zone that had once been her living room, Jessica sighed. "You have no idea how much that would mean to me."

"I'm glad to do it. Sometimes I miss not having a house full of girls."

"Bite your tongue," Pastor Walter's voice sounded in the background.

Jessica laughed. "What time did you want to pick up the girls?"

"I'll be there in half an hour. Oh, and, Jessica, word from the wise. Tell them to clean up their own messes so you can lounge while they're gone."

"I just might do that."

Jessica hung up the phone and surveyed the mass of art projects strewn across her table. There was no reason her girls couldn't clean up their messes. She liked Valerie's suggestion.

She cupped her hands around her mouth and hollered, "Girls, please come to the kitchen."

Maddie skirted in wearing a long dress-up gown. Her hair was plastered in twenty or more hair clips. Thick makeup covered her face. Izzy bounded down the stairs. A baby doll filled each arm and fluffy kitty slippers hugged her feet. Emily meandered into the room with the TV remote in her hand and a scowl on her face. Jessica fought the urge to chuckle. If her girls didn't exemplify the different stages of childhood, she didn't know who did.

She straightened one of Maddie's clips. "Valerie has offered to take you girls to dinner and a movie."

Three pairs of eyes glistened in delight. Jessica knew how much the girls loved to spend time with Valerie. She was the grandmother they'd never had.

"Here's the deal. You have to clean up all of your messes. She will be here in thirty minutes. If the house isn't picked up, you're staying home."

"We can do it, Mom." Izzy raced into the living room and scooped the Barbie dolls into her hands.

Maddie pushed Jessica out of the way and collected the craft material into a pile. "We'll be ready."

Even Emily meandered a little more quickly toward the stairs to start with the second floor.

Jessica laughed. "I didn't say I wouldn't help, but I will be watching to see if any of you wimp out and try to leave it all for me."

"We won't," Izzy and Maddie answered in unison.

Jessica fought her way through the battlefield of girl supplies and into the living room. She picked up the fort made of blankets covering the end tables, chair and couch. One by one, she folded until once again she could see a semblance of furniture.

"You made that mess!"

"No, I didn't!"

"Maddie, they're your dolls. I don't want to play with your old, ugly babies."

"I'm not picking them up."

Jessica stepped over the folded blankets and stomped toward the heated battle between Izzy and Maddie.

"They're your toys."

"Izzy, you did it."

"Mom, Maddie's acting like she's gonna hit me!"

Jessica hopped over a basket of play dishes. She'd need to get to them before they clobbered each other. She kicked aside a pile of dress-up shoes and then Maddie darted past her. Izzy followed close behind.

"Girls!" Jessica pointed her finger at the two of them just as her foot caught on a cord. With her balance gone, her body fell forward. She clutched for anything to break the fall. Her hand caught an afghan draped over the rocking chair. The motion didn't stop. Her hands braced for the fall. The impact was too strong. *Smack.* Her face hit the carpet. The afghan flipped and wrapped around her head like a protective covering. On its plunge to the floor, the chair hit her bottom and leg.

Jessica pushed herself up, knocking the chair onto its side. Her hands flailed at the afghan swarming her face. She puffed the stringy side threads out of her eyes. Several swiped her nose, sending her into a fit of sneezes. Finally she succeeded in ridding the unwanted headdress. She glared at the two culprits.

Izzy stood stiff with her hands clasped over her mouth. Her eyes were huge with surprise. Maddie's bottom lip quivered. Emily must have come downstairs to find out about the commotion, because she stood beside her sisters, hands covering her cheeks. Her mouth gaped open, big as the Grand Canyon.

"I cannot believe…" Jessica stood and sat the rocking chair upright. She picked up the afghan. Static electricity glued the blanket to her skin as she picked, pried and pushed the thing off her arms and onto the chair. She turned back to her daughters.

Merriment danced in Emily's eyes. Izzy's back heaved

in silent chuckles. A slight giggle slipped from Maddie's lips. She ducked her shoulders and covered her mouth.

Suddenly Jessica realized how ridiculous she must have looked boxing it out with the chair and blanket. And losing. A smile tried to form, but she bit her lower lip to keep the chuckles from escaping.

That proved too much for Izzy. She let out a small giggle. Laughter whipped through the room as each girl keeled over in guffaws. Jessica couldn't help joining their mirth.

Tears rolled down her cheeks. She swiped them away with her shirtsleeve. It felt good to laugh with them like this. Jessica was almost thankful for her sore bottom. She hugged each of her children and was surprised when Emily gave a slight hug back.

"All right, girls. We have to clean this up before Valerie gets here." She grabbed the pile of folded fort blankets. "No more fighting."

"Okay, Mom." Maddie leaned over and picked up a toy. She still had her hand cupped over her mouth. Air pockets of giggles escaped the sides.

In no time, Valerie arrived and collected the girls for their date. Jessica surveyed the clean house. She placed her finger across her lips. "Now what shall I do with myself?"

Excitement welled in her heart. She clapped. "I know exactly what to do."

She raced up the stairs, into her bedroom, and opened her nightstand drawer. She pulled out her sketch pad and pencils and clutched them to her heart. "I never have time for this anymore."

She skipped down the stairs and into the kitchen. Grabbing a soda and some chocolate candy pieces, she skittered into the living area and flopped onto the couch. She propped several throw pillows against the arm of the sofa, then leaned against them with her legs stretched out on the couch.

Snacks and supplies were laid on the floor beside her. The can snapped as she popped the top. She tossed a few pieces of chocolate into her mouth and bent her knees. She laid the sketch pad on her legs and stretched her arms toward the ceiling. "This is the life."

She picked up one of the pencils and touched it to the paper. The pencil seemed to sashay across the page of its own accord. A strong jawline appeared, then full eyebrows. She always drew things that pressed on her heart. She knew exactly who was forming on the page.

Dan parked in Jessica's driveway. She hadn't answered his text, but he knew she wouldn't mind if he took the girls for pizza. This time, he was determined to talk her into going with them.

He frowned when he saw the door ajar. Placing his hand on his gun, he leaned against the opening. He didn't hear anything. Slowly he pushed the door open enough so he could fit through. Thoughts of someone assaulting Jessica and the girls hurtled through his mind, and his heartbeat quickened.

Still, no sound. His gaze swept left and right. Nothing seemed unusual. The house seemed to be in order. So where were they? Jessica's van was parked in the driveway.

He tiptoed into the living area. Relief overpowered him when he saw Jessica. Her back was to him. Her legs were bent on the couch with her sketchbook resting on her lap. She was doodling in her pad.

"Jessica," he said, but she didn't respond. He noticed the cords connected to the headphones on her ears. Walking quietly toward her, he tried to decide the best way to announce his presence without sending her into a scared, screaming frenzy. He saw the picture.

It looked like…

He blinked and looked again. There was no mistaking it.

His image covered the page. Jessica was sketching his face. The detail of the drawing amazed him. She even included the freckle under his left eye.

Overpowering emotion filled his heart. She must have feelings for him. The kiss wasn't a mistake. A relationship between the two of them wasn't a crazy idea.

Her head cocked to the side as she flipped the pencil around and erased a few out-of-place lines. Then she lifted the pencil from the page and scratched the back of her head with it.

He backed up slowly. The best way to announce his presence was not to surprise her at all. He figured she'd die of embarrassment if she discovered he saw her drawing. He crept backward, one tiptoe at a time until he bumped into a small round table. A small cactus fell to the floor.

Jessica turned. Her gaze locked with his before she lost her balance. The pad flew through the air as she plunged to the floor. *"Dan!"*

She landed with a thump on the carpet, the pad following her. She scooped up the book and fumbled to a standing position. "What are you…"

They both glanced at the sketchbook with the sheet of his picture facing outward. Her face turned scarlet as she flipped pages. Dan placed the cactus back on the table but couldn't tear his gaze from her as she pushed stray strands of hair out of her eyes.

"Dan!" Her pitch was high. "What are you doing here?

A slow grin lifted the corners of his mouth at the scene that had just played out before him. No doubt about it. She must have feelings for him.

"I came by to…"

Her chin quivered. Tears pooled in her eyes. A tiny drop slipped down one cheek. Knowing he'd scared and embarrassed her, he crossed the distance in the room. His hand cupped her chin, and he swiped his thumb across the wet trail on her cheek. "I'm sorry, Jessica. I didn't mean to frighten you."

Jessica closed her eyes and swallowed.

"Your door was open. I was afraid someone might have broken in."

She sniffed the last trace of emotion away and opened her eyes. She didn't move away from him as she smiled. "What did you want?"

He sucked in his breath. What did he want? He wanted to cover her lips with his own. He wanted to press her cheek into his chest and hold her there for the rest of his life. He wanted to feel her arms wrapped around him.

"I wanted to take you for pizza."

Whew. He hadn't said anything crazy.

She narrowed her gaze and placed her hands on her hips. "Dan Robinson, how did you know I was home alone?"

He lifted his hands in surrender. "I didn't. I'd planned to invite the lot of you." He looked around the room. "Where are those girls anyway? Did you lock them up to get some peace?"

A hurt expression crossed her face.

Dan touched her arm. "I'm kidding. You know I love them as if they were mine."

Her eyebrows rose and her eyes widened. "You do?"

Dan's cheeks warmed. He looked at his hands, then clenched his fists at his sides. "Of course."

She didn't respond, and Dan searched his mind for what to say. She still stood so close he wanted to wrap her in his arms. "Will you go with me?" he asked.

Jessica stepped back and hugged the sketch pad to her chest. "Sure."

"Great."

"I'll just run upstairs and change."

She tripped over the rug. The pad flew through the air as she braced her fall with her hands. As quickly as she fell, she moved to a sitting position, then hopped to her feet. "Third time's the charm. There shall be no more falling for me today."

Dan chuckled as she ran up the stairs. He spotted the pad on the floor and clasped his hands. She'd forgotten to take it with her.

He looked at the pad for several moments. She hadn't meant to leave it. Wouldn't want him to look at it. The black book seemed to draw him closer. Jessica would prance down those stairs any second. She'd be furious if she caught him taking a peek.

Curiosity won the inner battle as he scooped it up and scanned the page with his portrait. His fingers traced the curves of the lines. The resemblance was uncanny. She had amazing talent. He flipped a few pages back. It was another picture of him. He was at a soccer field.

He thumbed to the next page. Him again. This time he sat between Izzy and Maddie at the dinner table. He scanned the pages; many of them bore his picture.

"Ready or not, here I come," Jessica called from the second floor. Dan laid the pad on the couch and stood.

She looked beautiful in a formfitting charcoal-and-cream-striped shirt. Plain matching slacks revealed her slight figure. A shadow draped her face as she glanced at the pad on the couch. "You looked at it, didn't you?"

Dan leaned back on his heels as he scratched his jaw. He couldn't lie to her. "I did."

Her face and neck burned red, and she turned away. "Please leave."

He grabbed her hand and nudged her back around to face him. "Jessica, let's talk about this. What are you afraid of?"

She narrowed her gaze. "I'm not afraid of anything. It's not right."

"Not right that you care about me?"

Jessica pursed her lips, and moments passed before she nodded.

"I understand how you feel. I promised Ryan to care for you and the girls."

"What do you mean?"

Dan sat on the couch and leaned forward, resting his elbows on his knees. Jessica sat in the chair across from him. He rubbed his hands together. "It all happened so fast that day. We went into the house. I could tell Ryan recognized the dealer."

He raked his fingers through his hair as he shook his head. "Ryan tapped his gun. That was our signal."

Jessica pressed her fingertips to her lips and wrapped her other hand around her middle.

Dan stared at her. He didn't want to talk about that night. Didn't want to relive what had happened. His heartbeat sped up. He could almost smell the stench of cigarettes and alcohol. "Shots and footfalls sounded through the room. I looked at Ryan. He was on the floor." He motioned to his stomach. "Covered in blood."

As he rubbed his thumbs against his fingers, it was as if he could feel his best friend's blood sticking to his hands. Could hear his partner's gasps. See Ryan's bloodstained shirt. "He wanted me to promise I'd take care of you and the girls. I said of course I would."

He couldn't look at Jessica. He stood and paced the

floor. "All this time I've beaten myself up over this." He rubbed his eyes. "How could I fall in love with my best friend's wife?" He trailed his hands down his cheeks and chin, until he clasped them and leaned his chin against his knuckles. "And yet that's what I did."

He braved a glance at her and saw confusion mixed with shock. She shook her head. "I don't understand. All this time?" She stared at him. "You just showed up two months ago."

Dan cringed. He hadn't planned to tell her about the monthly cash gifts like this. Blowing out a long breath, he sat on the couch and looked her in the eye. "I'm the one who's been sending you money."

She sat up straight and furrowed her brow. "I don't understand." She cocked her head and studied him until anger flashed through her eyes.

He clenched his fists. This night was not going as he'd planned. "I was going to tell you. I just didn't know how. I felt so guilty—"

"The birthday cards?" She pursed her lips.

Dan nodded slowly. Her mounting anger made him want to slither beneath the couch like a runaway snake.

"Christmas money last year?" She smacked her hands against her hips. "Was that you, too?"

"Yes," he admitted. He sat up straighter and spread his arms wide. "I've watched out for you all. I wanted to take care of you. To see to your needs and wants."

She stood. "I think you need to leave."

"Jessica, I was going to tell you. I love—"

She shook her head. "Please just go." She didn't wait for a response as she marched out of the room.

Knowing he wouldn't be able to convince her of anything tonight, he prayed God would open her heart to see how much he loved her and only wanted what was best for her.

He made sure the front door shut all the way as he left. After slipping inside his truck, he punched the passenger's seat. He should have told her the truth about the money when she'd asked weeks ago. No. He should never have fallen in love with her in the first place.

Chapter 13

Jessica turned the ignition. Nothing. She glanced at the bags of groceries in the back of the van. Turkey for Thanksgiving. Ice cream for the pies. Milk and orange juice. She opened the van door and fanned herself with her hand. "Even in the desert, it shouldn't be this hot in November."

"Miss Stephens says if it keeps up we'll have a record high," Izzy proclaimed as she kicked her legs against the back of the seat.

Jessica snarled. The woman had practically purred like a cat when Jessica shared Dan's number. She turned the key, trying again to start the van.

"It's dead, Mom."

Jessica rolled her eyes. "Thanks, Izzy."

"You're welcome," the five-year-old chattered. "Did you know a Western diamondback snake can shake its rattle sixty times a second?"

"I didn't know that." Jessica turned on her smart phone

and pressed Kim's phone number. The answering machine picked up. She tried Pastor Walter and Valerie. No response. She glanced at the groceries in the backseat, then stared at her phone again, willing one of them to call her back.

"Yeah, Miss Stephens says that's three thousand six hundred times a minute. That's a lot, huh, Mom?"

"That's a lot."

Izzy waved her hand in front of her face. "Mom, I'm getting hot."

Jessica bit her bottom lip. "I know, honey."

She closed her eyes. She didn't want to call Dan, but what choice did she have? He'd told her he loved her, and she'd kicked him out of the house. He probably wouldn't answer her call anyway. She stared at his number in the phone. He'd promised to take care of her and the girls.

Looking at the ceiling of the van, she suppressed a growl. He was going to get his chance again. She dialed his number, holding her breath until he answered. He sounded surprised when he said hello.

"Hey, Dan." She tapped her forehead, feeling like a complete heel. "My van won't start."

She remembered the last time the van had broken down. The bill had been paid. Right out of the blue. She balled her fist. By Dan, no doubt. "I'm at the store, and I've got groceries in the back. Ice cream and whatnot." Her voice cracked. "Just don't want it to melt."

"No problem. I'll be there in a couple minutes."

She put the phone on the passenger's seat, then looked at her reflection in the rearview mirror. Combing her fingers through her hair, she inwardly chided herself for worrying about what Dan thought of her appearance.

"Is Uncle Woolly coming to get us?" asked Izzy.

"Yes."

"Yay. Maybe he'll take us to get chicken nuggets. I bet Aunt Kim is getting some for Maddie, then Maddie'll come home and try to act like she's all special, but I'll tell her Uncle Woolly—"

She turned in her seat and interrupted her daughter. "Do not even consider asking him."

Izzy frowned. "Fine." She crossed her arms in a huff.

Jessica saw Dan's truck pull into the parking lot, and she waved at him. He nodded when he saw her and pulled up beside the van. Her heart pounded as he stepped out of the truck.

"Uncle Woolly," Izzy cheered.

He tousled her hair. "How you doin, Iz?"

"Did you know the saguaro cactus can live to be two hundred years old?" said Izzy as she climbed into the backseat of the truck's cab. "Miss Stephens told us that the other day."

Jessica bit her bottom lip. She hated the jealousy slithering through her each time Izzy mentioned her teacher.

"That's pretty cool to know," said Dan.

Jessica helped Dan move bags of groceries to the bed of the truck, then settled into the passenger seat. Her mind whirled with what to say. While Dan arranged the bags, she breathed in the pine scent of his car freshener, willing the relaxing smell to calm her nerves.

Dan hopped into the driver's seat. "I'll come back after I drop you off. See if I can get it started."

"You don't have to do that."

"Yes, I do."

She glanced at the man beside her. He didn't look her way. She opened her mouth to say…

"You're awfully quiet." He winked.

She clenched her jaw. So he planned to pretend nothing had happened between them. That he hadn't told her he loved her or that he hadn't admitted to sending her money and then not telling her when she had asked. "Just tired, I guess."

He patted her leg. "I'll have you home in a minute."

The humor in his tone irked her. He'd told her he loved her. Opened up his soul to her. The truth had set him free. Well, she loved him, too, but the consequences of succumbing to those feelings affected more people than just her.

She watched each building they drove past. The city seemed especially quiet tonight. A lone figure appeared a little ways ahead of them. The man wore a tattered shirt and a Razorbacks ball cap with a hole in the top. His shoulders were hunched over, but something seemed familiar about him. She peered out the window. She gasped and grabbed Dan's arm. "Stop. It's Frank."

"How do you know my dad?"

"We met him at the Reviewed Hope Center," said Izzy.

"Renewed," said Jessica.

"What?" Anger seeped through his voice.

"We're not going to argue about this right now," said Jessica. "Turn around and go get him."

"No."

"Why not? We'll take him to the center."

Dan's jaw set in a line. His knuckles turned white from gripping the steering wheel. "I will not."

Jessica hit the dashboard with her hand. "Yes, you will. How could you even consider leaving him out here?"

"You have no idea."

"You're right, but we're Christians, and the right thing to do is pick him up."

Dan looked away and rubbed his forehead. He turned the truck around. The few blocks back seemed to take an eternity. She could tell he was furious with her, but she didn't care.

Frank came into view. Dan stopped the truck, and Jessica hopped out in front of him, waving. "Hi, Frank. What are you doing?"

"Nothing much. Just moseying around." He grinned, exposing his rotting yellow teeth.

She didn't smell alcohol on his breath, so she wrapped her arm around his. "Come on, stranger. We'll take you to Betsy's."

Frank smiled and looked at the truck. He frowned and pointed at Dan. "Don't think he's wanting to take me anywhere."

Jessica gritted her teeth. "Doesn't matter. You're coming with us."

Frank got into the truck, and Jessica climbed in after him. "Thank you, son."

Dan didn't respond.

They didn't speak as they drove to the Renewed Hope Center. Jessica yearned to knock some sense into Dan. She didn't doubt Frank had been a bad father, but how could Dan just leave him on the streets? His actions didn't make sense. He'd taken care of her and the girls in ways she probably still didn't know, but he held so much anger for one man.

After dropping off Frank, Jessica and Izzy, Dan raked his fingers through his hair, upset. Jessica could never fathom how much anger he felt for his dad, what it was like to grow up with a drunk for a father and a drug addict for a mother. Yes, Jessica had lost her mother, but she'd grown up in a middle-class home with a dad and sister who loved her.

He jumped out of the truck and bounded up the walk to

his apartment. Childhood memories swarmed his mind. Some days, he'd come home from elementary school and no one would be there. He'd run around to the back of the complex and dig up the spare house key from underneath a rock. His parents would be gone for hours. He'd fix peanut butter and jelly sandwiches for dinner and fall asleep on the couch watching television. Some nights, he didn't know if they even came home.

And yet Jessica wanted him to help the man who had never cared for him, had never loved him. Frank had had his chance. Dan shouldn't have to help him. His focus was on people with whom he could make a difference. Jessica. The girls. Randy. Randy could change. Frank couldn't. Dan kicked off his shoes and flopped onto the recliner. "She has no idea what she's asking."

He scooped up the remote, turned on the television, then surfed through stations. Sports. Drama. Cartoons. Nothing appealed to him. Her words replayed in his mind. *We're Christians, and the right thing to do is pick him up.*

He shifted in the chair. People said things like that when they hadn't experienced the pain themselves. Unable to sit still, he walked into the kitchen and grabbed a soft drink from the refrigerator. He stepped out onto the back deck and leaned against the railing. Looking up at the dark star-dotted sky, he wondered how God was able to forgive so quickly and freely.

His inability to forgive his father wasn't all that bothered him. Jessica thought less of him as a Christian. Dan sought to be a man of integrity. Someone people trusted. Especially Jessica and the girls. And he'd seen the disappointment in her eyes.

The phone rang, and he walked back into the apartment. Seeing Jessica's name on the screen, he debated answering. He didn't want to listen to her harass him about not wanting to help his dad. But if she needed something…

He picked up the phone and pressed Talk. "Hello."

"Dan, I'm sorry."

The sincerity in her tone soothed the ache in his heart.

She continued. "I don't know what it was like to grow up with an alcoholic father. I've seen some of the guys challenge Betsy at the center." Her voice caught. "You're one of the kindest, most wonderful Christian men—"

"Okay," Dan interrupted her. "That's enough of that."

"I shouldn't have said the things I said."

"I forgive you." The words came out easily, and he meant them. But then, forgiving someone for saying something hurtful was a lot easier than forgiving someone for a wrecked childhood.

He remembered how his youth minister, Vic, had shown him in scripture how God could make good from anything. He thought of Randy. They had a connection because Dan understood his life.

"You are coming over for Thanksgiving, right?" Jessica asked.

"Am I invited?"

She sniffed. "Of course you're invited. The girls would wring my neck if you didn't come over."

"Even Emily?"

She chuckled. "Yeah. I think she wants you to come, too."

"Then I wouldn't miss it for the world. What time? What do I bring?"

"Four o'clock, and just yourself is great. See you tomorrow."

"Definitely."

Someone knocked on the front door as he ended the call. Dan opened it. "Randy?"

The teenager shuffled back and forth. "Whatcha doin'?"

He motioned him into the apartment. "Drinking a Coke. Watching some TV."

Randy walked in and rubbed the back of his neck as he looked around. "Nice place."

Dan didn't have a lot of decorations, but he had a great couch and recliner and a top-of-the-line television. He nodded. "Serves a bachelor well. So, what's up?"

Randy shrugged. "Just wonderin' if I could crash with you awhile."

He studied the kid. "Sure. I'll just call your mom and let her know you're here."

"You don't have to. Her new *boyfriend* took her on a vacation for the holidays."

Dan tilted his head back. Now he understood. Randy didn't want to be alone for the holiday. He knew the feeling all too well. Dan tapped his phone. "I'm still gonna call her cell and leave a message. In case she comes home early and wonders where you are."

Randy's deadpan expression assured him that wasn't likely to happen.

Dan pointed to the refrigerator. "Get yourself a drink. Something to eat if you're hungry while I give her a call."

As Randy walked into the kitchen, Dan noticed the drawstring bag on his back. Most likely, a change of clothes. Dan was getting the opportunity to make a difference in a young boy's life. He had empathy for Randy because he'd been through the same things. *Nothing's wasted,* Vic had said time and again. Maybe one day he would be able to forgive his dad.

Chapter 14

Jessica opened the can of apple pie filling and dumped the contents into the already-made piecrust. She sprinkled sugar and cinnamon on top, then spread the mixture with a butter knife and placed another piecrust on top. After fixing a second pie using the same method, she placed them on a cookie sheet and shoved them into the oven.

She wiped her forehead with a paper towel. "That's as close to homemade as my pies will ever get!"

A chuckle rose in her throat. Pastries had always been a weakness to her taste buds, but an evasion to her cooking abilities. She assumed that was God's blessing on her hips.

"However—" Jessica pulled the ingredients for her famous sweet-potato casserole from the cabinets "—this I can make."

"Mom, who are you talking to?"

Jessica turned and found Izzy with her head cocked to the side and a perplexed expression on her face. She nestled the child close. "Just talking to myself. Happy Thanksgiving."

"Happy Turkey Day." Izzy ran to the table, grabbed a chair and dragged it toward the cabinets. "Can I help?"

"Sure can." Jessica handed her the measurement of brown sugar. "Dump this in the bowl while I mash the yams."

"Mom, Miss Stephens said that in Arizona it's illegal for donkeys to sleep in the bathtub. Did you know that?"

Jessica tapped Izzy's nose. "Sounds like a good law to me."

Maddie walked on tiptoes into the kitchen with her nose high in the air. "I can smell the turkey."

"Smells good." Izzy licked her lips.

Maddie pointed to the bowl. "I wanna help, too."

"I know you do." Jessica pulled another mixing bowl from the cabinet. "Which is why I'm assigning the green bean casserole to you."

Maddie scrunched up her nose.

Jessica handed her the opened cans of green beans and pointed to the cream of mushroom soup. "You don't have to eat it. Just mix it together."

"Are we gonna make sugar cookies?" Emily asked from behind her.

Jessica looked back at her oldest daughter and motioned her into the kitchen. "Of course. What kind of Thanksgiving would it be if we skipped that tradition?"

"Things have changed quite a bit."

Jessica nodded. "The last two Thanksgivings have been very different."

"And sad," Emily added.

"Sad moments," Jessica agreed. "But not entirely sad."

As Emily gathered the ingredients for the cookies, Jessica thought of the guests she expected for dinner. She could only pray Dan would be up for her surprise guest.

The four of them kept busy through the morning and into the afternoon, stopping long enough for a little bit of lunch. The front door opened, and they heard the clicks of Kim's shoes against the tile floor. "We made it."

Frank walked into the kitchen and whistled. "Look at all the food."

Izzy raised her hand. "I made the sweet potatoes."

"And I did the green beans," said Maddie.

Frank moved closer to Emily. "What about you, girlie?"

Emily shrugged. "Little bit of everything, I guess."

Frank pointed to the red-and-green-iced cookies. "Mmm. I haven't had a sugar cookie in years."

"Knock yourself out," said Emily.

Frank grabbed a cookie and popped the whole thing into his mouth. While he oohed and aahed, Jessica leaned closer to her sister. "He looks good today."

Kim nodded. "He smells pretty good, too. I was nervous about bringing him over here."

Jessica swatted the air. "He's not going to cause any problems."

Kim placed her hand on her chest. "No. It's because I didn't want to bring him over here by myself."

Jessica wrinkled her nose. "I guess a solo ride might be a little awkward."

"Yeah." She bobbed her head. "But, as it turned out, he was great. Betsy said he's been talking about coming all week."

"We just need to pray the rest of the company is okay with him being here." The doorbell rang, and Jessica lifted her pointer finger. "On that note…"

"He's here." Kim grinned. "Better go answer the door."

Jessica pressed the wrinkles in her dark capris, then peeked in the foyer mirror to be sure her hair and makeup were okay. She opened the door, and her heart flipped at the sight of Dan all spiffed up in a freshly pressed, button-down maroon shirt and khaki pants. His clear blue eyes drew her, but she focused on sharing her guest list before any potential scenes.

"Dan, I'm so glad you're here." She opened the door wider. "I have a surprise. I need you to keep an open mind."

"I was thinking the same thing." Dan moved to the side. A young man stood next to him. "Jessica, this is Randy Mullins. Randy, this is Mrs. Michaels."

Her stomach dropped and twisted into a knot. She looked at Dan. He seemed to be holding his breath. His eyes begged her to let him explain further. Sucking in a breath, she extended her hand to the teenager. "Hello, Randy. I've seen you in the lunchroom."

A blush crept up the boy's neck and over his ears as he shook her hand. The kid didn't seem that bad in person, and she'd simply have to trust that Dan had a reason for bringing him. Besides, she had her own surprise to share with Dan.

"Randy?" Emily's voice sounded breathless from behind Jessica. "Hi."

"Hi, Emily." Randy shoved both hands in his front pockets and looked at his feet.

Jessica motioned the guys into the house, noting the relief in Dan's gaze. She chuckled. "Remember, we're keeping an open mind."

"What?"

"I have a surprise guest, as well."

Frank walked out of the kitchen. "Hello, son."

Dan's expression fell, and he narrowed his gaze at the man. "What are you doing here?"

Jessica placed her hand on Dan's chest. She pulled it away as if she'd touched fire. "I invited him."

Dan didn't speak, but he frowned and clenched his jaw.

Frank walked back into the kitchen, and Jessica turned and poked Dan in the chest. "What is the matter with you?"

"It's not your place—"

"Yes, it is." Frustration boiled within her as she whispered, "I can invite who I want to my own house. I did not do this for or against you. This has nothing to do with you. I wanted to have Frank as my Thanksgiving guest." She raised her index finger in the air. "That's why he's here." She balled her fist and stomped her foot.

Dan's eyes searched Jessica's in challenge, but she determined not to budge under his scrutiny.

"I don't plan to talk to him," Dan snapped.

"That's your loss."

Silence blanketed them. Her shirt felt tighter, and her breathing became more labored, but she refused to allow him to win this battle of wills.

A smile cracked the edges of his mouth. "You got spunk, little lady."

Offended, Jessica squared her shoulders against the man twice her size. "I'd appreciate it if you didn't call me that."

Without warning, Dan lifted her off her feet and twirled her around as he would have nearly two years ago as Ryan's best friend—the girls' uncle Woolly. Tonight, though, he didn't feel like Uncle Woolly. He stopped and held her close to his chest longer than necessary. His gaze drifted to her lips.

Jessica gulped. What could possibly have caused this change in emotion?

Her blood burned as his cheek brushed against hers. Tingles shot down her back. His breath tickled her ear. "I guess we both received a bit of a surprise," he said.

Jessica's body went limp. He placed her feet back on the floor, but she fell against the sofa. Insisting her muscles regain functional ability, Jessica stood to her full height. "Yes. I suppose you're right."

The oven timer beeped.

"I…I believe the tur…turkey's ready." She inwardly berated herself for stammering.

Pure satisfaction shone on Dan's face.

She rolled her eyes and mumbled, "I'll never understand the male ego."

"Excuse me?"

Jessica chuckled and widened her eyes in mock innocence. "Nothing. Just talking to myself."

Dan sighed in relief. Aside from lovesick-puppy looks exchanged between Emily and Randy and an occasional comment from Frank, dinner had gone well.

Jessica clapped her hands. "Okay, girls, let's clear the table."

"We're gonna watch football, right?" asked Frank.

"Absolutely," said Jessica. "I mean, if you want to."

"I'll watch football with you, Mr. Robinson," said Randy.

"Me, too," added Emily.

Dan noted the protective gleam in Jessica's eye and said, "You better help your mom with dishes first."

"But we always get the Christmas stuff out," whined Izzy.

"We still can," said Maddie. "Right, Mom?"

"Sure," said Jessica. "We won't put it up until tomorrow, though."

"Come on, girls." Kim stood and picked up several dishes. Emily followed her aunt's lead.

"Are you gonna put the outside lights up this year?" asked Maddie.

"Yeah." Izzy scrunched her nose. "It wasn't the same last year without them."

"I don't know." Jessica picked up a casserole dish in each hand. "I don't really know how to get them up."

"I'll help," said Dan.

Her expression, both refusing and pleading, drew him, and he wished he could scoop her up and plant a kiss right on her lips.

"Yeah!" Izzy exclaimed. "Uncle Woolly would know how to do it."

Maddie hopped up and wrapped her arms around his neck. Izzy jumped up and joined her. With both girls squeezing the life out of him, he murmured, "I'll be here first thing in the morning."

Jessica nodded. "Okay."

The girls released his neck and raced into the kitchen to start the dishes.

Frank stood. "Think I'll head into the living room for that football I was talking about, if you don't mind."

"I'll go, too." Randy followed him out of the dining room.

Dan had a feeling the boy wanted to get away from Jessica's suspicious glances more than he wanted to watch football. Emily touched her mom's arm and stuck out her lip in a pout.

Kim leaned close to Jessica and whispered, "Let the girl sit with her boyfriend."

Jessica scowled. "Fine." She pointed at Emily. "But there had better be plenty of space between you two."

Emily nodded repeatedly, then gave her mom a quick hug. When the young teenager left, Kim said, "Sometimes you're a bit too hard on her."

"I am not." Jessica looked at Dan. "Am I?"

He lifted his hands. He didn't want any part of this discussion. They'd had a pleasant visit, and he preferred it stay that way. "I plead the Fifth."

Jessica put the dishes down and placed her hands on her hips. "If you want to be the big caretaker of this family, you need to have an opinion."

Kim's mouth formed a perfect O. "What's this? Is there a disagreement between the lovebirds?"

"Kim!" exclaimed Jessica.

Her sister sighed. "Ugh. Let's just stop playing games. It's obvious you care about each other." She flipped her wrists. "Just say it already."

Dan lifted his eyebrows and winked at Jessica. He'd said his piece. She knew how he felt.

Jessica grabbed up the dishes again and strode to the kitchen. "Honestly."

Kim looked at him. "She'll get there. We're close."

Dan wrapped his arm around her in a side hug. "I always knew I liked you."

He picked up dishes and took them into the kitchen. While Kim and Jessica put leftovers in Tupperware dishes and Maddie and Izzy washed and dried, Dan wiped off the table and counters. In no time, the kitchen was clean.

They headed into the living room. Jessica stopped, and Dan looked past her at the couch. Emily and Randy sat alone holding hands. He kissed her. A quick kiss, but a kiss just the same. Why had two teenagers been left alone? Dan looked around the room. Where was his dad?

"What do you think you're doing?" asked Jessica.

Emily and Randy jumped apart.

Frank stepped out of the bathroom. "A little kiss never hurt nobody."

Dan glared at him. "What is the matter with you? Why did you leave them alone?"

"A man's gotta go to the bathroom every once in a while," Frank retorted.

Jessica grabbed Dan's shirt and pulled him back into the kitchen. "You shouldn't have brought Randy here."

Her words cut through him. She wasn't giving the kid a chance.

"He's trying to change."

"I think it's time for you and Randy to go home."

Dan started to argue, but dropped his hands to his sides. "Fine. I'll drop my dad off at the center."

"I never said Frank had to leave."

Dan gawked at Jessica. "He just made a joke about them kissing, but you want *him* to stay."

Her cheeks darkened in anger. "This is my house. I will do what I want."

"Fine!" Dan stalked out of the kitchen and motioned for Randy. "Come on. We're going back to my place."

Randy shook his head. "I'm sorry." He turned to Emily, who had tears streaming down her cheeks. "I'm sorry, Em."

As they walked back to the truck, the teenager shook his head. "I shouldn't have kissed her. It was just once. Just a quick kiss."

Dan looked at the kid in the passenger seat beside him. He was a typical eighth-grade boy. They shouldn't have kissed, but it was Dan's dad, the adult, who'd left them alone. Jessica infuriated him. She was determined to help the wrong person.

Chapter 15

Christmas music pealed through the truck's radio as Dan drove to Jessica's house. They hadn't spoken since their post–Thanksgiving-dinner argument. She might not want him to come over today, but he'd said he'd help put up the Christmas decorations. And when he said he'd do something, he did it.

Jessica was already outside untangling the lights when he pulled into the driveway. She offered a quick wave. "Thought you might not come."

"I said I would."

Jessica tapped one foot. "I guess I overreacted a bit last night."

"Just a bit?"

"I didn't expect to see my thirteen-year-old daughter sitting on the couch swapping spit with some boy."

Dan crinkled his nose.

Jessica grimaced. "That sounded gross, didn't it?"

"I think, overall, the kiss was fairly innocent."

She shuffled her feet. "I know. Kim keeps warning me that I'm pushing Emily away. I just want to protect her."

"And you're doing a great job." He pointed to the outside lights. "Looks like we have our work cut out for us."

Jessica grimaced. "Ryan was a Christmas-light fanatic."

"I remember." He chuckled. "I helped him put these up every year."

They separated the lights, then checked that each strand worked. After changing a few bulbs, Dan hung the colored icicle lights around the roof while Jessica worked on setting up the candy cane lights along the front walk. Once they were finished, Dan hung large lights around the archways and windows. Jessica arranged the prelit Christmas tree and plastic Santa and snowman.

Jessica wrapped her fingers around his biceps. "I think you've earned a break, Mr. Robinson."

Dan followed her into the house. She poured glasses of sweet tea, and they plopped into chairs opposite each other. He picked up a napkin from the center of the table and wiped his forehead. "Every year I wanted to choke Ryan for putting up so many lights."

"Are they ready?" Izzy squealed.

"I bet they are," Maddie said.

The girls raced outside. Emily followed at a slower pace. Jessica swallowed a drink of the tea and pointed to the yard. "That's why."

"And the girls are definitely worth it."

"You wanna stay and help put up the Christmas tree?"

A sense of belonging enveloped him. He hadn't realized how much he longed for a family. Alone most of the time as a kid, he'd just grown accustomed to doing his own things. Ryan had been his one good friend, someone he'd have done anything for, but he'd never considered himself part of their family. He placed the glass on the table. "Let's do it."

They dragged the enormous box into the living room. Dan set the bottom half of the artificial tree on its base, then popped the top half into place. While he and Jessica spread and arranged branches, the girls rummaged through the container filled with ornaments.

"Look, Mom, I made this one in first grade." Maddie showed them a felt cactus decorated with sequins and glitter.

"Here's one Aunt Kim bought me," said Izzy as she held up a clay smiling face with yellow yarn for hair.

"Remember this?" Emily clutched a small red frame. Inside was a picture of their family when Izzy was a newborn.

Izzy giggled as she pointed to the baby. "Is that me?"

"Sure is." Jessica took the picture and stared at it. "Doesn't seem possible that was five years ago."

Feeling like the outsider, Dan stood and wiped his brow. "Phew, this is hard work. I need another drink of that tea."

He walked into the kitchen, then gripped the back of a chair. He could never replace Ryan. Didn't even want to. He missed his friend, and yet he loved Jessica. The two were a direct contrast.

"I'm glad you're helping Randy."

Dan turned at the sound of Emily's voice. She opened the cabinet and took out a glass.

She continued, "He told me about the bad things he's done. How he's on probation."

Dan's gut twisted in a knot. She was too young to know about such things. Jessica was right that Emily didn't need to mess with boyfriends at only thirteen. And though he cared about Randy, Dan knew Emily shouldn't get caught up in all the things the boy was dealing with.

"I don't know why he decided to tell me the truth," she said. "At first, he'd told me the rumors were lies, and I believed him."

Dan searched his mind for what to say. Neither she nor Randy needed to be worried about a boyfriend-girlfriend relationship. Both of them had plenty to deal with in their individual lives.

She poured tea into her glass and took a drink. "I shouldn't have let him kiss me last night."

Dan nodded. "That's right. You've got plenty of time before you need to worry about boys."

"But I'm glad you're helping him. He's a nice person." She cocked her head. "And did you know he's really smart?"

"I found that out not too long ago."

"When you helped him try out for basketball?"

"Yes. I guess he told you about that."

Emily nodded. She placed her glass on the table and headed back toward the living room. She stopped but didn't turn back around. "At first I blamed you for letting Dad get shot, but I know it wasn't your fault, and I'm…I'm glad you're here."

She walked out and Dan lifted his gaze to the ceiling and sent a silent praise to God. He couldn't take Ryan's place, but he could make a place of his own. He'd won over the girls. Now to convince Jessica.

Jessica followed her sister into the nail salon. She couldn't remember the last time she'd had a pedicure and manicure, but she intended to enjoy every minute of this one. The lady guided them to two chairs, and Jessica kicked off her sandals. She sat down, pushed the button to turn on the automatic massage and pressed her back against the chair. "This feels wonderful."

"I know. I'm addicted," said Kim. "Dan's got the girls?"

"Yeah. Said he wanted to take them Christmas shopping."

"For you, I'd suppose."

"Probably."

Jessica closed her eyes, letting the warm water around her feet and the automatic neck and back massage transport her to a place of serenity.

"I think he loves you," said Kim.

"He's already told me he does."

"What?"

Jessica startled when Kim leaned forward and lightly pinched her leg. "He's told you he loves you?"

"In a way, yes. He hadn't meant to say it, but he did."

Kim punched Jessica's thigh. "What is the matter with you?"

"What do you mean?"

"I know you love him."

Jessica opened her mouth, but Kim held up her pointer finger. "Don't even try to deny it. I've known you way too long."

Jessica lifted her hands. "What does it matter if I do?"

Kim frowned. "What does that even mean? Of course it matters."

"But Ryan—"

"Ryan loved you. If he could choose, he'd probably handpick Dan to—"

"Don't say take his place."

Kim shook her head. "No. Make a new one. Don't you think Ryan would want you to be happy? To find love again?"

In her heart, Jessica knew he would. The guilt she felt for caring for Dan had subsided over the past months. Plus, the girls adored him. Even Emily had softened.

"It's not just that," she said, and flinched as the pedicurist touched the bottom of her foot. Jessica covered her face to keep from laughing. Pedicures were terrific, but they also tickled.

"Then what is it?" Kim demanded.

Her sister obviously wasn't going to drop the subject. Jessica waited until the woman stopped tickling her and started filing her toenails. "It's Frank, too. How can he be so mean about his own father?"

"You don't know everything that Frank has done to tear apart their relationship."

"I know, but you can't just give up on a person who needs the Lord."

"Randy needs the Lord."

Jessica sat up straight and glared at her sister. "What are you trying to imply?"

"I'm saying take the plank out of your own eye before you start messing with the splinter in someone else's."

Jessica sucked in a breath and crossed her arms in front of her chest. She looked away from her sister. How dare Kim turn the situation on her? Make it about Randy? Jessica had every right to want to keep that boy away from her house. He was a bad influence on Emily. A drug dealer, for crying out loud. He'd even kissed her daughter in her house after she'd told the two teenagers to keep space between them.

"Listen, Jessica, I'm not trying to make you mad."

"Well, you're not doing a very good job."

"Truth is," Kim went on, "you both need to give a little. Emily called me last night…."

Jessica's chest tightened. "She did?"

"Yeah. She'd just gotten off the phone with Randy. Told him she wanted to be friends, that she wasn't ready for a steady boyfriend."

Jessica's heart ached. "Why didn't she tell me?"

"Because she thinks you hate him." Kim shrugged one shoulder. "And let's face it. Remember when we were kids? When Dad was determined we weren't going to do something, we'd try to do it anyway."

"I remember."

"You've got to keep the boundaries. You're right she doesn't need to date him. But you've got to listen to her if you want her to listen to you."

Jessica leaned her head back and allowed the rolling of the automatic chair to loosen the muscles in her shoulders and neck. She let Kim's words seep into her pores. Keeping her eyes closed, she said, "When did you get so smart, little sister?"

"I had an awesome big sister."

Jessica opened one eye and smiled at Kim. She reached over and squeezed her sister's hand. "I'm really glad you asked me to come with you today."

"Me, too. Hey, we *are* going to the Surprise Party Holiday Festival this weekend, right?"

"Don't we every year?"

Kim wrinkled her nose. "I might not be able to go with you on Friday night."

"Why?"

"I might have a date."

Jessica clasped her hands. "Really? Spill it."

"It's just a new guy at work."

"College or law office?"

"Law office."

"Christian?"

"Of course."

"Handsome?"

"Definitely."

Jessica clapped her fingertips together. "I am so excited. When can I meet him?"

"Well, it's just a first date. Let's not creep him out."

Jessica's jaw dropped and she pressed her hand against her chest. "Are you calling me creepy?"

"No, but meeting the whole family on a first date sounds like a woman on a mission to get married."

"Isn't that the truth?"

Kim leaned forward. "We don't have to tell him that."

They laughed, and Jessica said, "I really do hope it works out."

"Me, too." She flipped her wrist. "Maybe you should invite a date to go with you and the girls to the festival."

Jessica grinned. "Maybe I should."

Chapter 16

When they arrived at the entrance of Surprise's annual holiday festival, Dan, Jessica and each of the girls placed a bag full of nonperishable groceries in a box labeled Operation Santa. Dan brimmed with happiness. He, Jessica and the girls would enjoy the hot air balloon glow, the Arizona Seahawks Skydivers demonstration, live entertainment and snacks. In the past, he'd worked the event as an off-duty officer, but he'd never attended with a family.

Izzy wrapped her hand around his and guided him to the edge of the roped-off area containing the hot air balloons. "The rainbow-colored balloon is my favorite."

"I like that one," said Maddie. She pointed to a balloon shaped like a mushroom with a red-and-white-polka-dotted top. The stem showed a smiling boy opening shutters next to a buzzing bee.

"That's pretty cool," Dan agreed.

Izzy pouted. "You don't like mine."

He tweaked her nose. "The one you like is cool, too."

"One of these days I wanna go up in one," said Emily.

Jessica lifted her hands and shook her head. "Not me. I'm terrified of heights." She pointed to the basket of one of the hot air balloons. "You wanna fly around in the sky in that?"

Emily grinned. "Looks like fun to me."

"Me, too," said Izzy.

Maddie cringed. "I think I'm with Mom."

A band played upbeat music from the stage and people began to gather where the Arizona Skyhawks Skydivers would land. The cool evening air brushed against Dan's cheeks. Jessica buttoned Maddie's sweater. Following her lead, he zipped up Izzy's jacket. Jessica smiled at him, and he fought off the urge to grab her hand.

"I see some friends from school," said Emily. "Can I go talk to them?"

Dan looked at the group. Several girls. A couple of boys. None of them looked to be doing anything unsafe or bad. Jessica worried her bottom lip. He knew she struggled with allowing Emily more freedoms. "How about for half an hour?" He tapped his phone. "Then you call your mom to check in."

Emily lifted her eyebrows and looked at her mom, her eyes begging consent. Jessica nodded. "Sounds good. Don't forget to call."

After giving her mom a quick hug, Emily waved to the group and raced over to them.

Jessica sighed. "It's hard watching her grow up."

Dan wrapped his free arm around her shoulder. "I know."

She leaned her head against him, and he nestled her closer.

Maddie pointed to the sky. "I think it's about time for the Skyhawks."

Izzy jerked his hand. "Let's get closer."

He released Jessica's shoulder, and then dared to take her hand. She didn't pull away as they walked toward the open space for the skydivers. Within minutes, the crowd cheered when three lights blazed through the sky. Moments passed, and they could see the men and their parachutes. The girls squealed when the skydivers landed on their feet and bowed to the crowd.

Jessica's phone buzzed. She talked to Emily a moment, and then placed it back in her pocket. With a sigh, she looked up at Dan. "She's going to stay with her friends while the hot air balloons go up." She grabbed Dan's hand. "I'm glad you're here with me. My heart is beating a hundred miles a minute knowing my child isn't within arm's length of me."

He wanted to be with her. Tonight. Tomorrow. For the rest of their lives. He held her hand tightly as they meandered in the direction of the hot air balloons.

"Is that Aunt Kim?" Izzy asked.

Jessica jumped. "Where?"

"I see her." Maddie pointed at the stage. "By the band."

Jessica released his hand, wrapped her arm around his, pressing close to him. "Yep. That's her."

"Who's she with?" asked Izzy.

Dan saw the blond-haired man standing beside the girls' aunt, but all he could concentrate on was the floral scent of Jessica's perfume and the closeness of her lips as she whispered in his ear, "That's her date."

He couldn't stop himself. In one swift motion, he captured her lips with his. Her eyes widened in surprise, and she looked down at the girls. Neither of them saw them, but he still could have kicked himself for acting on the impulse.

He wanted to kiss her. Had replayed in his mind more

times than he could count the one kiss they'd shared in the police station. But he didn't want stolen kisses. He wanted them to be given.

Attempting to ease the tension, he said, "You wanna go say hi to them?"

Jessica blinked several times. "No. Let's wait until she's ready to introduce him." She took hold of his hand again. "Besides, I think these girls want to see the balloons, right?"

"Yeah!" Maddie and Izzy cheered.

He relished the feel of her hand in his as they followed the girls. She'd taken hold of his hand. She'd also captured his heart.

Jessica had thought about Dan all night. How he'd handled Emily. The feel of his hand wrapped around hers. Their brief kiss. Even now she couldn't get him out of her mind as she and Kim and the girls walked back to the holiday festival for another day of fun and games.

"Let's go to the camel rides," said Izzy.

Maddie shook her head. "No, the merry-go-round."

"The merry-go-round's closer," said Jessica. "We'll do that first."

Izzy frowned and stomped her foot, but Maddie grabbed her hand and tugged her forward. "Come on. It'll be fun."

Emily pulled a few dollars out of her purse. "Can I go get some cotton candy?"

"Sure. Just meet us at the ride," said Jessica.

Kim raised her eyebrows. "Letting the girl walk alone."

Jessica motioned toward the concession stand. "I can see her from here."

"Still. This is a big step for my overprotective sister."

Jessica hefted her purse strap higher on her shoulder. "You're not kidding, but I'm trying to give a little space.

Show a little faith." She elbowed her sister lightly. "So, tell me about your date."

Kim bit her bottom lip as she hugged herself. "It was great."

"We saw you."

"You did? Where?"

"Standing beside the band. He's cute."

Kim closed her eyes. "I know."

"I don't think I've ever seen my well-polished, lawyer/professor sister so excited." Jessica laughed.

"It's like I'm a teenager again." She shook her head and pointed to Emily at the concession stand. "And I never want to go through those years again."

Jessica lifted her finger in the air. "I'll second that."

A giggling Maddie and Izzy ran back to them. "We saw the face painting," Maddie said. "Can we do that next?"

"Can we, Mommy?" asked Izzy.

Before she could answer, Emily appeared beside her. "Want some?" She offered the green cotton candy to her sisters and both girls yanked off pieces.

Surprised, and proud, Jessica smiled. "I'm fine with face painting next," she said, watching her girls eat the sticky treat.

"Maybe your mom and I will even do it," said Kim.

"What?"

"Yeah, Mom," Maddie laughed. "You do it, too."

Jessica glanced at her oldest daughter. "Only if Emily gets one, as well."

Emily shrugged. "Why not?"

They made their way to the face-painting stand. Maddie chose pink-and-purple butterfly wings to go around her eyes. The artist drew a soccer ball with flames on Izzy's cheek. Emily decided on a yellow flower design that curved around her right eye.

"Which one are you going to get, Jessica?" Kim asked.

"I kind of like this one." She touched a red heart outlined in black and white with little curls drawn along the top and bottom.

Kim pointed to several designs. "You don't want a Christmas tree or a Santa."

Jessica smiled. "I kinda feel like a red heart."

Her sister leaned close. "So your date went well, too."

"I wouldn't call it a date."

Kim wrinkled her nose. "Sis, you've got three kids. Yesterday was your kind of date."

Jessica slugged her sister's arm, and then turned to the woman doing the face painting. She pointed to the heart and sat still while the woman completed the job. Once done, Jessica glanced at Kim's face. "You got the same as me."

Kim grinned. "We both had a good date."

They followed the girls over to the pony and camel rides. When they passed the petting zoo, Izzy insisted they go through it first. Jessica's nose wrinkled. The girls didn't seem to mind the stench drifting from the area, but the smell was not appealing to her.

Oh, well. The girls would smell like camels for the rest of the day anyway once they rode one.

Jessica was reaching past the fenced area to pet the goat when someone tapped her shoulder. She jumped, pressing her hand against her chest. She glared up at Dan, but good-naturedly. "You scared the life out of me."

Mischief lit his eyes as he grinned. "Sorry 'bout that."

She planted a hand on her hip. "You don't look very sorry."

"Hey, Randy," Emily said beside her.

The teenager had emerged from behind Dan. He glanced from Jessica to Emily and waved, then shoved his hand in his pocket. She fought the urge to grab Emily's hand and drag her away from the boy who'd had the nerve to kiss her in Jessica's own home. Forcing a smile, she said, "Are you two having fun?"

"We are," said Dan. He studied her, probably trying to figure out if she was going to pounce on his protégé. "Randy has never been before."

"Really?" Emily's eyebrows lifted. "We're getting ready to do the camel ride. You wanna hang out with us?"

Randy smiled. "Sure."

Jessica's heartbeat sped up and her chest tightened as the two of them walked beside Izzy and Maddie.

Kim nudged Jessica's arm. "Did you hear that? She asked him to join 'us,' not go off by themselves. She's such a good girl."

Jessica glanced at her sister and smiled. "You know what works on me, don't you?"

"I've had a few years of practice." Kim glanced at Dan. "Need any pointers?"

Dan grinned. "I might."

Kim extended her arm, and he linked his through it. They walked behind the kids. "What are a few good tips?" he asked.

Jessica pursed her lips. They thought they were as funny as the clowns walking around the festival. As if on cue, a man dressed in a candy cane costume jaunted past her on a pair of stilts. A Christmas tree and another candy cane followed behind him. Shaking her head, she joined her family at the animal rides.

"You wanna ride an elephant with me?" Dan asked.

Jessica touched her chest. "Me? On one of those things?" She gestured at the ginormous gray mammal. "Weren't you there last night when Maddie and I admitted our fear of heights?"

Dan touched her elbow. "I won't let you fall."

The sweetness in his eyes melted her heart. She might be willing to try anything if he looked at her with such sincerity. "Okay."

Kim gasped. "Really?" She punched Dan's arm. "I take back everything I said. You've got her in a whole different playing field than the one I'm familiar with."

Jessica scowled at her sister as she and Dan got in the elephant-ride line. She waved to her girls and Randy as they rode by on their camels. She was pleased to see that Izzy rode with Emily and Maddie rode with Randy. The line grew shorter until she and Dan were next. Her hands grew clammy. "I'm gonna regret this."

"You'll be fine," he whispered in her ear.

His closeness sent a soothing balm through her. The elephant guide helped her onto the saddle, if that was what it was called, and soon Dan was behind her. She leaned back into him and focused on his arms wrapped around her waist and his breath blowing her hair. The ride ended too quickly. The air seemed cooler when she was out of his embrace. She missed the safety of his arms.

Chapter 17

Jessica scooped up a glob of butter and smoothed it on the Italian bread. She shook garlic salt on top, and winced as a tiny pain shot through her side. Jessica arched her back and stretched her neck. She enjoyed helping Betsy at the Renewed Hope Center, but with the busyness of the Christmas season, she'd almost wished she could have stayed home and vegetated on the couch.

The girls would never let her miss an opportunity to be here. Without a doubt, God used this place to help bring about the changes she'd seen in Emily. And Betsy was thrilled to have them. She even paid the girls five dollars each when they completed their chores.

Betsy trudged into the kitchen with a load of sheets in her arms. Jessica wiped her hands on a towel, then reached out to take the load. "Here, let me help you."

"No. You finish the garlic bread." Betsy scooted away from Jessica. "Izzy, Maddie and I are heading upstairs to change the bedsheets. Just take the baked spaghetti out of the oven in ten minutes."

Her two youngest daughters appeared from the laundry room with linens piled high in their arms. Jessica chuckled at the sight of Betsy, Izzy and then Maddie scaling the stairs like ducklings following after the mama duck.

"How are you today, girlie?" Frank's voice boomed from the dining room where Emily was setting the table.

"Fine."

"Just fine? Where's the little spitfire I met several weeks ago?"

Jessica peeked into the dining area and saw Frank poking Emily's shoulder.

Her daughter frowned. "Stop it, Frank."

The man lifted his arms in surrender. "I ain't doing nothing." He scratched his partly grown beard with his fingers. "You oughta know by now I'm just picking at ya."

"Well, don't pick at me. It's annoying."

Frank backed away. "Fine, fine." He leaned against one of the dining room chairs. "How's that young fellow of yours doing?"

Emily turned back to the table and finished setting the plates and utensils. "You mean Randy?"

"Why, yeah."

"He's good. We're just friends now."

Frank cackled and swatted his leg. "Your mama make you break up?"

"No. It was me."

The timer above the stove buzzed. Jessica grabbed the pot holders and pulled the baked spaghetti from the oven. She placed a pan of garlic bread inside and set the timer for ten minutes. The doorbell rang, and she hustled to the front door. She opened it and gasped. "Dan?"

He rubbed his hands together. "You have no idea how

hard this is for me." He raked his fingers through his hair. "But…" He nudged Randy to his side and dropped his arm on the teenager's shoulder. "You didn't trust Randy around Emily because he'd made some bad choices…"

Randy looked away and shuffled his feet. He didn't stiffen up or deny Dan's words. Jessica's opinion of the boy grew.

Dan continued. "You're giving the boy a chance." He blew out a long breath. "We've come to help out. I'm going to try to give Frank a chance."

Joy swelled in Jessica's chest as she pulled them both into the center. She wrapped Dan in a big hug, and then, though she felt uncomfortable, she hugged Randy, too. "Betsy always has a ton of work for us to do."

"What's that, you say?" The older woman padded down the stairs. She smiled and shook Dan's hand. "How are you doing?"

"I'm okay. How are you doing, Betsy?"

"The good Lord's keeping me good as always." She grabbed Randy's hand and squeezed it between both of hers. "Did I hear someone say I've got two more helpers?"

Jessica nodded and touched the boy's shoulder briefly. "This is Randy."

Betsy smiled. "It's nice to meet a handsome young fellow willing to help others out."

Randy's face turned bright pink, but Betsy kept hold of his hand and guided him into the dining area. Jessica and Dan followed.

"Well, if it isn't Kissy Face," Frank howled when they walked into the room.

Jessica bit her tongue and touched Dan's arm when she felt him tense beside her. "I'm going to give Dan a chore outside."

"Sounds good to me," Betsy cooed.

"See ya around, son," bellowed Frank.

Before Dan could say anything, Jessica dragged him through the kitchen and out the back door.

In the yard she pressed her hands against his cheeks. The bristles of his beard poked her fingers and she traced her fingertips along his jaw. The fire in his eyes shifted as the intensity of his gaze fell to her lips.

Rising on tiptoes, she intertwined her fingers around his neck as he wrapped his arms around her waist. He lowered his lips to hers, and tingles shot down her spine. He cupped her cheeks in his hands and looked her in the eye. "I love you, Jessica."

Her breath caught. "I love you, too."

Tears welled in her eyes as the admission fell from her lips. He kissed her again, wrapped strong arms around her, smashing her against his chest. "I've waited so long to hear you say that."

Jessica giggled and maneuvered out of his embrace. Hurt filled his eyes, and she slugged his arm. "I couldn't breathe."

Dan laughed as he lifted her up and twirled her around in one of his old hugs. He placed her back on her feet, and she tugged at the bottom of her shirt to straighten it. "There is a valid reason why the girls call you Woolly Mammoth."

He flexed his biceps. "I'm a big guy."

"Vanity!" Jessica chuckled and punched his arm again. "And yet it's true."

Dan kissed her lips again. "You better give me a job quick, or I'm not letting you leave."

Jessica debated which she preferred.

The next week, the middle school gymnasium was packed with Eagles fans. Parents and kids in navy-and-orange sweatshirts and shirts filled the bleachers. Cheerleaders bounced and flipped from the sidelines. Instruments honked and clanked as the band warmed up. The buttery, salty smell of popcorn made Jessica's mouth water.

Memories washed over her. She and Ryan had met in school. High school, not middle school. Still, the atmosphere was similar. She remembered holding hands, watching ball games and sneaking kisses when no one was looking.

Dan led her and the girls to an empty row in the middle of the bleachers. Emily motioned to a group of girls near the front. Then she skittered away to the giggling bunch.

Jessica watched the teams warm up on each side of the court. Randy seemed to be a good player, making most of his layups. He saw them in the stands and his face lit up. Compassion for him grew in her heart.

"I'm going to get some sodas and popcorn. Do you want anything?" Dan asked.

Izzy raised her hand as if in class. "I do."

"Me, too," added Maddie.

"All right." He rubbed both their heads. "You two come with me. Mom, you want a Coke?"

Jessica blinked at his address. She'd heard couples do that all the time, address each other as Mom and Dad. She'd always thought it odd, but hearing it from Dan... somehow it made her feel as if they were a team. Mom and Dad raising the kids together. "Sure. Coke sounds great."

While they were gone, the coaches called the boys back to the benches. The band began a drumroll, and the announcer stood. "Welcome to the home of the Mighty Eagles!"

The fans screamed and stomped their feet. The noise was deafening, but intoxicating. She saw Emily out of the corner of her eye, and Jessica's heart swelled as she watched her daughter clap and giggle with her friends.

"The Prestonville Panthers' starting lineup…"

The crowd hushed as the names of the archenemy were called. At least for tonight, they were mortal foes. Only a handful of Panthers fans had traveled the hour to cheer for their team—faithful parents and a squad of cheerleaders—but they yelled and squealed loudly as the team's starters made their way to the center of the court.

A drumroll thundered. "And now for the Eagles…" Whistles and cheers, stomps and claps shook the walls of the gymnasium.

Jessica leaned forward. Anticipation mounted. The atmosphere must have gotten the best of her, because she was ready to cheer on her school's boys. Specifically, she hoped to hear Randy's name.

When their names were called, one boy and then another slapped hands with teammates as they ran to the middle of the court.

"At guard," the announcer's voice boomed. "Randy Mullins."

Jessica jumped, extended her arm, made a fist and shook it in the air. "Yes!"

Surprised by her excitement, she sat back on the bleachers and looked around to see if anyone had seen her. No one seemed concerned by her display.

The whistle blew. The referee launched the ball in the air. The Panthers' center got the tip. Randy swiped the ball from the player and dribbled to the basket for an apparent shot. He faked the defender and threw it back to another boy, who made an easy three pointer.

Cheers erupted. Jessica jumped and clapped. She was proud of the boy and how far he had come.

"That was an awesome play." Dan and the girls wiggled back into their seats beside her with candy, popcorn and sodas.

"Yes, it was." She grabbed a handful of popcorn and shoveled it into her mouth. "You should be proud of him."

"I am."

The first quarter had nearly ended when Jessica realized Randy hadn't taken a shot. He had chances, and she'd seen him shoot well during warm-ups. She leaned closer to Dan. "Have you noticed Randy never shoots?"

"I had."

"Wonder why."

"I don't know."

Emily bounded up the steps with two friends trailing behind her. "Mom, can I get a drink?"

Jessica reached into her purse, but Dan already held money out to her. "Just bring back the change."

"You got it, Pops." Emily scooped up the money and raced down the bleachers.

Hearing her call him Pops seemed weird. She glanced over and saw Izzy had both arms wrapped around his leg and her head resting just above his knee.

Jessica nudged him. "I could have given her money."

He shrugged and focused on the game.

She loved Dan. She wanted the girls to love him. They should see him as their father figure. Ryan would want that. And yet she felt as if they had forgotten their dad. A year and a half had passed, and life had moved on.

Without Ryan, the man she'd promised to love, honor and cherish forever.

Until death do you part.

The end of their vows crashed against her chest. She wasn't wrong to love Dan. Nor were the girls. But she still felt…weird. Like cheating. Or going back on her commitment. Would she always have moments when she felt like this?

Trying to push her conflicting thoughts away, she focused on the game again. By the end of the third quarter, the Eagles barely held the lead, but Randy still hadn't taken a shot.

The fourth quarter winded down. Ten seconds left. The game tied. One of the kids dribbled the ball toward the net. Randy was open. The boy glanced at him, then to his other players. All were blocked. All but Randy. For some reason, the kid wouldn't pass. He took a shot, and the ball bounced off the rim. Two seconds left. Randy jumped for the rebound. He clutched the ball in his grasp, then shot it into the basket. The bullhorn sounded to end the game.

Fans jumped in wild excitement. The players cheered. Except one. The boy who wouldn't pass the ball marched over to Randy. Jessica gasped when he took a swing. Fury wrapped Randy's expression, and he punched the boy. The kid fell back, and Randy jumped on top of him.

"Mommy, what's he doing?" cried Izzy.

The coach and kids pulled Randy off the teammate, but Jessica couldn't watch any more.

She gripped Maddie and Izzy by the hands. Both girls had tears in their eyes. Thankful she hadn't ridden with Dan, she said, "I gotta go."

"I'll check on him. Find out what happened."

"I'd prefer not to know."

She bounded down the steps and yelled for Emily to join her. They got in the van. Emily sniffed. "I don't know why Andy took a swing at Randy."

Jessica looked at her daughter. "It appeared to me that Randy got the best of that other kid."

"I know, Mom," Emily whined. "But didn't you see Andy during the game? He was being a jerk. He wouldn't pass. He pushed him a couple times. It was Andy's fault."

Jessica clamped her lips shut as she looked in the rearview mirror. Both of the younger girls cried quiet tears.

Randy had scared them. Raising children wasn't a game. It wasn't something she could do over if she messed up. She was keeping her girls away from bad influences like Randy Mullins. Dan Robinson, too, if necessary.

Chapter 18

Dan knocked on Jessica's front door. When she opened it, he smiled at how pretty she looked in a Christmas-green sweater and blue jeans. He held up an envelope. "Your monthly gift."

Jessica frowned. "I don't think that's funny."

"I'm not messing around. I'll help you and the girls from now until forever."

She crossed her arms in front of her chest.

"And I already know the girls are with Valerie and that you're planning to go Christmas shopping. I'm going with you."

She curled her lip. "What are you, a stalker?"

"Stalker? No. Protector? Definitely, yes." He placed the envelope in her hand. "Get your jacket and come on."

"I don't have a jacket. I need to get one."

"Then grab your purse and let's go."

She didn't say much as he drove her van to the toy store.

He didn't know what had upset her so much the other night at the game. Aside from Randy's fight. Which it was obvious the other guy had started. Not that Dan and Randy—and the coach and the other kid's parents—didn't discuss what needed to happen the next time the boys had a disagreement. Both boys had been disciplined.

Whatever upset her, it was more than Randy's fight. She'd been tense and frazzled before that. He and Jessica had shared a great time at the center, some terrific kisses, too, and then something had gotten under her skin.

Before the day ended, he'd get to the bottom of it. They got out of the van, and Dan grabbed a cart to push through the toy store. One thing he knew for certain, women were a tough lot. And four of them. He raked his fingers through his hair. He wondered if he'd end up bald, or at the very least gray.

After he followed Jessica around for a few hours, they finished shopping, and Dan placed the last bag of toys in the back of the van. He got in the driver's seat. "Now where?"

"The mall."

Once inside the shopping center, Dan took hold of her hand. She didn't let go, and his heart swelled. Whatever had her upset the other night, they would work through it.

"Let's go in there." Jessica pointed to a department store with her free hand.

"Sure." He liked shopping about as much as he liked completing paperwork after an arrest, but he'd go for Jessica, and he'd be happy while he was there.

She guided him through rack after rack of juniors' clothing. Bored to the core with teenage girl garments, Dan focused on the woman he wanted to make his wife. She was only three years younger than him, but she looked twenty-something. Penetrating, ocean-blue eyes held him captive with a glance. Shiny blond hair warmed him like the sun.

He nodded his approval for the red sweater she'd selected for Emily, then tapped the top of the clothes rack and looked around the store. He wondered what Jessica would look like in that sweater. Or maybe in green. No. Blue. She'd be breathtaking in blue. "Stop it," he mumbled.

"What?"

Unwilling to admit his wandering thoughts, he patted his belly. "Stomach's growling. I'm hungry."

"Oh."

Her mouth formed a perfect O, tempting Dan to give her a kiss. *I think she's doing it on purpose, Lord.*

"Let's pay, then just one more store."

She led him into a jewelry store, where she picked out a silver bracelet for Emily.

"Those are really pretty," he said. "Let me get you one."

Jessica stared at the bracelet and didn't respond.

He touched her arm. "What's the matter? Something was wrong at the ball game. It was more than just Randy."

Jessica rolled her eyes and looked up at him. "I know. Randy's fight..." She shook her head. "I was so mad and determined to keep the girls away from his influence, but that wasn't what was wrong."

"What is it, then?"

She stared into his eyes. "I love you, Dan. I do."

He rubbed her upper arm. "I'm glad to hear that. Please, tell me what's wrong."

"It was when Emily called you 'Pops.'"

Understanding began to dawn on him. "You felt like she was taking away from Ryan."

Jessica nodded. "Yeah." She twisted her diamond stud earring. "And I know Ryan would want you to be a dad to the girls. He's probably in heaven right now cheering for you."

Dan cupped Jessica's chin with his hand. "It's okay to feel that way. You just need to talk it out with me, not shut down."

"You're right."

He picked up a silver bracelet for Jessica. "Now, let's go pay for these."

The school's winter break had begun. The girls would have new toys and games to occupy them after Christmas, which was only a few days away, but for now, the girls had gotten antsy. Jessica decided a trip to the roller rink might be just what they needed. As they laced up their roller skates, the scent of salty nachos and popcorn tickled Jessica's nostrils. Even though she'd fill up on Christmas foods and treats for the next two weeks, she was determined to sample some of the skating rink's snacks before they left.

A disco ball hung from the center of the ceiling, casting bright sparkles on the otherwise dark rink. Kids skated forward and backward in groups of twos and threes. An older boy raced around the rink showing off his moves.

Emily spied a couple of friends and waved goodbye to Jessica and the younger girls.

"Guess it's just us," said Jessica.

"You gotta hold me tight." Maddie grabbed her arm.

"Me, too," said Izzy.

"I will."

Jessica guided the girls onto the rink. They held her hands as they skated the large circle. Soon Maddie's confidence built, and she released Jessica's hand and skated ahead. Izzy held on tightly.

"Don't let me go," she begged.

"I won't."

Maddie skated past them and lifted her hands. "Look, Mom."

"You're doing great."

"Mommy, I'm thirsty." Izzy yanked on her arm and then slipped, but Jessica caught her.

She looked at the clock. An hour had already passed. "All right. Let's get a drink."

"And nachos?"

"Sure."

Jessica guided Izzy back to the tables, then waved to the other girls. Emily and Maddie skated to them, and Jessica gave Emily money to purchase some snacks.

The music stopped, and a woman with long blond hair skated to the middle of the rink. She twirled on her skates, then lifted the cordless microphone to her lips. "It's time to limbo."

Heat flamed Jessica's cheeks. She loved to limbo.

A catchy tune blasted over the speakers. Two teenage boys set the limbo's base and stick in place. Skaters cheered and rolled toward the middle of the ring.

"Come on, Mom." Emily shuffled her eyebrows. "You wanna do it with me? You used to be good."

Jessica bit her bottom lip. She looked at Maddie and Izzy, who both nodded for her to go. She glanced back at Emily. "You know I want to."

She and Emily skated to the center of the rink. Most of the participants skated under the first two notches of the limbo stick with no trouble. Some of the children were short enough they didn't even have to duck.

By the time the stick was lowered another notch, Jessica had to push her shoulders and head back to skate beneath it, but she made it. She waited for Emily to make it through, then she high-fived her daughter.

Two more notches down, and Emily bumped the rod and it fell to the floor. She looked back at Jessica when the boys placed the stick back on the base. With a thumbs-up, she cheered, "Come on, Mom. You can do this."

Jessica didn't even care about the silly limbo game. She praised God that He'd restored a good relationship between her and Emily. Her oldest daughter seemed more healed every day. Still, she gave Emily a thumbs-up as well, then focused on the limbo contraption.

After a deep breath, she raced for the stick. The wind pushed strands of hair from her face. She arched her back to clear the stick. Her chest caught the rod, and it fell to the ground with a thud. She scrunched her nose as she skated back to the girls.

"I thought you were going to win, Mommy." Izzy grabbed her hand.

"So did I."

Jessica turned at the sound of Dan's deep voice. Heat rushed to her cheeks as she noticed the merriment dancing in his eyes.

"You're pretty flexible," he said.

"I can't believe you saw that."

He laughed, and Jessica shook her head. Everywhere she turned, Dan was there. Always watching over her and the girls. Even at embarrassing moments, she was glad to see him.

Dan tried to focus on the Christmas Eve service, but Jessica was entirely too distracting. He kept thinking about how cute she had looked skating with the girls. And doing the limbo.

His plans for the next day pounded his mind. The delicious scent of her perfume assaulted him. And wouldn't you know the slit in her long black skirt would be on his side? Not a big slit, just enough to open below the knee, but he couldn't stop glancing at her calves and her feet in those black high heels.

He took a deep breath and zoomed in on Pastor Walter. Sounds came out of the man's mouth. Dan was pretty sure he was even saying words, but for the life of him, he had no idea what they were.

Jessica leaned over and whispered, "I hope the girls heard what Pastor Walter just said."

Her minty breath made his stomach flip. He would like to have heard the man, as well.

Jessica poked his leg. He glanced at her, and she raised her eyebrows and nodded.

Dan had no idea what the pastor had said. All he could think about was Jessica, and how he wanted to scoop her soft hand into his.

That was it. He stood and quietly walked down the aisle to the restroom. He turned on the faucet and splashed cold water on his face. "Help me, Lord. Help me focus."

He wiped off with a paper towel, then closed his eyes, taking several deep breaths. He'd go back into the sanctuary, but he'd sit in the last pew. He'd tell Jessica he didn't want to disturb anyone. It was a feasible excuse.

He opened the door and bumped into a youth heading into the restroom. "Excuse me."

The teenager looked up at him.

"Randy?"

"Hi, Dan." Randy lowered his gaze, shoved his hands in his front pockets and shuffled his feet.

"I'm glad you're here." Dan patted the boy's shoulder, then engulfed him in a quick hug. "I thought you were with your mom. Who brought you?"

"I walked."

"From your apartment?" Dan stepped back and surveyed the kid. "Awful long walk in the cold. Your house is several miles from here."

"It wasn't so bad."

"How 'bout I give you a ride home after the service?"

Randy shrugged. "Okay."

He cupped Randy's shoulder with his hand. "Come on. We'll go find a seat together."

The boy didn't move. Instead he swiped his eye with the back of his hand.

Dan frowned. "What's the matter, son?"

"Will you tell me how to be a Christian?"

Dan swallowed the knot in his throat and blinked back his own tears as his youth minister's face flooded his mind. He'd been a difficult teenager with a chip on his shoulder just like Randy, but Vic had made a difference in his life. He cleared his throat.

Randy's face paled. "What's wrong?"

He wrapped the boy in a hug, then led him to a place where they could talk. "Outside of the day I accepted Christ as my Savior, this might be the proudest day of my life."

Chapter 19

"This one's for you." Izzy handed Dan a box wrapped in silver paper with a red bow on top.

"And this one," said Maddie. She gave him a smaller gift wrapped in green paper.

He watched as the individual piles of presents for the girls got bigger and bigger. He looked at Jessica. "I don't remember buying this many presents."

Kim piped up. "Some are from me." The bell on her elf hat tinkled as she bobbed her head. She lifted a pointy brown, felt-covered foot in the air. "I'm one of Santa's elves, you know."

Izzy puckered her face. "You are not."

Kim pulled her ear. "Just kidding." Then she looked at Dan and Jessica and brushed her forehead with the back of her hand.

"Where's the one for Mom?" asked Maddie.

Dan cringed as he worried which present the eight-year-old was referring to. He pointed to her stack. "She's got a bunch right there."

Maddie shook her head. "No. The little one."

Emily hopped up and grabbed a small present from under the tree. "You mean this one?" She placed the present in Jessica's pile.

"No. The one from Uncle Woolly," she whispered in a voice the whole neighborhood could hear. "The one he told us about."

Dan glanced at Jessica. Thankfully she was busy helping Izzy read his handwriting on one of the presents.

Emily grabbed Maddie's arm, then covered her lips with her pointer finger. "That's not till later. It's a surprise, remember?"

Maddie opened her mouth in a large O, then giggled and sat beside her stack of presents. Once everything was passed out, Dan took in the scene before him. He'd never seen anything like it. Each girl had ten presents or more. He and Jessica and Kim had half as many.

"Are you ready?" said Kim.

"Not yet." Jessica picked up a camera from the end table. She clicked several shots.

"Come on, Mom," whined Izzy.

"Everyone smile first."

The girls smiled with their mouths, but their eyes showed their desire for her to stop taking photos.

"On my three," said Kim.

Dan sat up. "Wait a minute. What's on your three?"

"Complete and utter chaos," Jessica mumbled.

"One…two…three."

Dan sat back in his chair as the three girls ripped through their gifts. Giggles and bows and shreds of paper flew through the air. They didn't even look. Just ripped and laughed. Within minutes, the shredding stopped.

Emily let out a whistle. "Okay. Let's see what we got."

This time, the girls opened boxes and examined toys and outfits. Emily squealed over the bracelet her mom had picked out. Izzy loved the doll he and Jessica had searched hours for, and Maddie could barely contain herself when she saw the butterfly costume.

Kim and Jessica opened their gifts. When Jessica opened the jacket he'd bought her, she gasped and tried it on right away. The brown leather looked good on her. It would protect her from the cooler temperatures, just as he would protect her and the girls as long as there was breath in his body.

When his turn came, he opened a Razorbacks ball cap, a couple of shirts, a clay police figurine and several ornaments and magnets made by the girls. Jessica pulled one more present out from under the couch and handed it to him. "I made this for you."

He tore off the paper and lifted the top of the box. Inside was a drawing of his face. A true likeness. Around the picture, she'd drawn smaller symbols to represent him. A cross. A badge. Two people shaking hands. A heart. A basketball. An envelope. He looked up at her and grinned when he saw the envelope.

"This is amazing, Jessica," he said.

"Thanks." She touched the eyes of the drawing. "I spent a lot of time on the eyes. Getting them as kind as yours." She rested her hand on his. "Words can't express how thankful I am for you."

Dan held his breath to keep from saying all he wanted to say to her. Kim must have seen the dilemma on his face, because she hopped up. "I think it's time for breakfast. Anyone else hungry?"

"I am." Izzy stepped over boxes. "But I'm taking my dolly with me."

"My stomach's growling," said Emily.

"Mine, too!" Maddie jumped up from the carpet.

Jessica followed the girls. "Let me take the breakfast casserole out of the oven. It should be warm enough by now."

When they'd left the room, Kim patted his head. "Keep a lid on it, Woolly Mammoth. You'll get your moment in a couple of hours." She winked.

Dan leaned his head back against the chair. A couple of hours were too long.

Jessica hustled to the oven and turned off the beeping timer. She slipped on the oven mitt and pulled out the cake. She could hardly believe Randy had accepted the Lord on Christmas Eve, and then Dan had told her the boy's birthday was Christmas Day.

It pained her that his mother didn't mind him leaving their apartment on Christmas, on his birthday, for an impromptu surprise celebration. And yet she was thrilled to spend time with him. She selected chocolate icing and sprinkles from the cabinet, then counted out fifteen candles from several boxes.

"Can I help?" asked Emily

"Sure, get in here. Where are your sisters?"

"Playing with their gifts." Emily grinned. "Aunt Kim's playing, too."

"She'll always be a kid at heart."

"Yeah, but did you know she's leaving in a couple hours?"

Jessica nodded. "To go to Brock's house to meet his parents."

"Seems so weird for Aunt Kim to have a boyfriend."

They saw less of Kim since she'd gotten serious with Brock. Even though her absence was another change, Jessica was happy for her sister.

Once she finished icing the cake, Emily arranged the candles and wrote Randy's name with the tube of red icing. Her daughter looked at her. "I'm glad Dan went to pick up Randy and Frank. It's good everyone is getting along."

"Yes, it is."

Emily leaned against the counter. "I like Dan. I think Dad would be glad he's here for us."

Jessica's lower lip quivered. "I think you're right."

The doorbell rang, and Jessica glanced at the kitchen clock. "They're half an hour early. Hurry, get Kim and your sisters and hide." Jessica shooed her out of the kitchen, then walked to the front door. "Just a minute."

She checked to be sure each of her girls and Kim had found a place to hide and bit back a laugh as she twisted the knob and opened the door.

Dan stepped into the room with red balloons in one hand and a bouquet of red roses in the other. In unison, everyone yelled, "Surprise!"

"What…" Jessica placed her hand on her chest to slow her racing heart.

"Fooled ya, didn't we?" Frank waltzed in behind Dan carrying a bakery box. He stuck out his thumb and pointed to Randy. "Just so ya know, it *is* his birthday, though."

Jessica placed her hands on her hips. "What is…"

Dan leaned down and kissed her lips.

Heat rushed her cheeks. "Dan Robinson, what are you—"

"It's a surprise, Mom." Emily grabbed her forearm. A smile covered her face.

Jessica frowned. She had no intention of kissing their uncle Woolly until she'd had a chance to talk with them. "Girls—"

"It's okay, Mom," said Emily.

Jessica furrowed her brow.

"For crying out loud," Frank said, grinning. "Just read the cake."

"Wait!" Dan yelled.

It was too late. She'd already read it. Marry Him was written in red letters on pure white icing. A big red arrow pointed to the right. Exactly where Dan stood.

Jessica looked at Dan.

An impish grin spread across his face.

Jessica stared at Kim and the girls. "Did you all know about this?"

"He asked us the day we went shopping," said Emily.

A chuckle slipped from Jessica's lips. She playfully punched Dan's arm. "I can't believe you pulled this off."

He shrugged, blue eyes dancing.

"I mean, how in the world did you get Maddie to keep the secret?"

Maddie giggled and pumped her fist through the air. "I did it. I kept a secret."

Kim, Emily and Izzy high-fived her.

Dan handed the flowers and balloons to Emily. "Is that a no or a yes?" He grabbed Jessica's hands and closed the gap between them.

His hands shook. They were cold, yet sweaty. He was obviously nervous. She released his hands and wrapped her arms around his waist, peering up into his eyes. "You and your dad seem to be getting along well," she whispered.

"Yes." He lowered his face and his short beard scratched her forehead. "But that wasn't my question."

She lifted her face until her lips almost met his. "I love you."

"Does that mean yes?"

"Yes."

Dan captured her lips with his and lifted her into the air, twirling her until she felt dizzy. He released her lips, but held her close to him. "I can't wait to take care of my girl." He placed her back on her feet, glanced at the onlookers and grinned. "All my girls."

Jessica held him tightly. Touching him, holding him, loving him, freely, openly, felt more wonderful than she had imagined. She reached up one hand and brushed his cheek. "You promise?"

"Oh, Jessica."

He wrapped burly arms around her in such sweet tightness she feared she'd lose her breath.

Dan kissed the top of her head, then lifted her chin until their gazes met. "I promise."

* * * * *

REQUEST YOUR FREE BOOKS!

2 FREE INSPIRATIONAL NOVELS
PLUS 2
FREE
MYSTERY GIFTS

Love Inspired

YES! Please send me 2 FREE Love Inspired® novels and my 2 FREE mystery gifts (gifts are worth about $10). After receiving them, if I don't wish to receive any more books, I can return the shipping statement marked "cancel." If I don't cancel, I will receive 6 brand-new novels every month and be billed just $4.74 per book in the U.S. or $5.24 per book in Canada. That's a savings of at least 21% off the cover price. It's quite a bargain! Shipping and handling is just 50¢ per book in the U.S. and 75¢ per book in Canada.* I understand that accepting the 2 free books and gifts places me under no obligation to buy anything. I can always return a shipment and cancel at any time. Even if I never buy another book, the two free books and gifts are mine to keep forever.

105/305 IDN F49N

Name _____ (PLEASE PRINT) _____

Address _____ Apt. # _____

City _____ State/Prov. _____ Zip/Postal Code _____

Signature (if under 18, a parent or guardian must sign)

Mail to the Harlequin® Reader Service:
IN U.S.A.: P.O. Box 1867, Buffalo, NY 14240-1867
IN CANADA: P.O. Box 609, Fort Erie, Ontario L2A 5X3

Are you a subscriber to Love Inspired books
and want to receive the larger-print edition?
Call 1-800-873-8635 or visit www.ReaderService.com.

* Terms and prices subject to change without notice. Prices do not include applicable taxes. Sales tax applicable in N.Y. Canadian residents will be charged applicable taxes. Offer not valid in Quebec. This offer is limited to one order per household. Not valid for current subscribers to Love Inspired books. All orders subject to credit approval. Credit or debit balances in a customer's account(s) may be offset by any other outstanding balance owed by or to the customer. Please allow 4 to 6 weeks for delivery. Offer available while quantities last.

Your Privacy—The Harlequin® Reader Service is committed to protecting your privacy. Our Privacy Policy is available online at www.ReaderService.com or upon request from the Harlequin Reader Service.
We make a portion of our mailing list available to reputable third parties that offer products we believe may interest you. If you prefer that we not exchange your name with third parties, or if you wish to clarify or modify your communication preferences, please visit us at www.ReaderService.com/consumerschoice or write to us at Harlequin Reader Service Preference Service, P.O. Box 9062, Buffalo, NY 14269. Include your complete name and address.

LIDIR13R

REQUEST YOUR FREE BOOKS!

2 FREE RIVETING INSPIRATIONAL NOVELS
PLUS 2 FREE MYSTERY GIFTS

Love Inspired®
SUSPENSE

YES! Please send me 2 FREE Love Inspired® Suspense novels and my 2 FREE mystery gifts (gifts are worth about $10). After receiving them, if I don't wish to receive any more books, I can return the shipping statement marked "cancel." If I don't cancel, I will receive 4 brand-new novels every month and be billed just $4.74 per book in the U.S. or $5.24 per book in Canada. That's a savings of at least 21% off the cover price. It's quite a bargain! Shipping and handling is just 50¢ per book in the U.S. and 75¢ per book in Canada.* I understand that accepting the 2 free books and gifts places me under no obligation to buy anything. I can always return a shipment and cancel at any time. Even if I never buy another book, the two free books and gifts are mine to keep forever.

123/323 IDN F5AN

Name	(PLEASE PRINT)

Address	Apt. #

City	State/Prov.	Zip/Postal Code

Signature (if under 18, a parent or guardian must sign)

Mail to the Harlequin® Reader Service:
IN U.S.A.: P.O. Box 1867, Buffalo, NY 14240-1867
IN CANADA: P.O. Box 609, Fort Erie, Ontario L2A 5X3

**Are you a current subscriber to Love Inspired Suspense books
and want to receive the larger-print edition?
Call 1-800-873-8635 or visit www.ReaderService.com.**

* Terms and prices subject to change without notice. Prices do not include applicable taxes. Sales tax applicable in N.Y. Canadian residents will be charged applicable taxes. Offer not valid in Quebec. This offer is limited to one order per household. Not valid for current subscribers to Love Inspired Suspense books. All orders subject to credit approval. Credit or debit balances in a customer's account(s) may be offset by any other outstanding balance owed by or to the customer. Please allow 4 to 6 weeks for delivery. Offer available while quantities last.

Your Privacy—The Harlequin® Reader Service is committed to protecting your privacy. Our Privacy Policy is available online at www.ReaderService.com or upon request from the Harlequin Reader Service.
We make a portion of our mailing list available to reputable third parties that offer products we believe may interest you. If you prefer that we not exchange your name with third parties, or if you wish to clarify or modify your communication preferences, please visit us at www.ReaderService.com/consumerschoice or write to us at Harlequin Reader Service Preference Service, P.O. Box 9062, Buffalo, NY 14269. Include your complete name and address.

LISDIR13R

REQUEST YOUR FREE BOOKS!

2 FREE INSPIRATIONAL NOVELS
PLUS 2
FREE
MYSTERY GIFTS

Love Inspired.

HISTORICAL

INSPIRATIONAL HISTORICAL ROMANCE

YES! Please send me 2 FREE Love Inspired® Historical novels and my 2 FREE
mystery gifts (gifts are worth about $10). After receiving them, if I don't wish to receive
any more books, I can return the shipping statement marked "cancel." If I don't cancel,
I will receive 4 brand-new novels every month and be billed just $4.74 per book in the
U.S. or $5.24 per book in Canada. That's a savings of at least 21% off the cover price.
It's quite a bargain! Shipping and handling is just 50¢ per book in the U.S. and 75¢ per
book in Canada.* I understand that accepting the 2 free books and gifts places me under
no obligation to buy anything. I can always return a shipment and cancel at any time.
Even if I never buy another book, the two free books and gifts are mine to keep forever.

102/302 IDN F5CY

Name	(PLEASE PRINT)	
Address		Apt. #
City	State/Prov.	Zip/Postal Code

Signature (if under 18, a parent or guardian must sign)

Mail to the Harlequin® Reader Service:
IN U.S.A.: P.O. Box 1867, Buffalo, NY 14240-1867
IN CANADA: P.O. Box 609, Fort Erie, Ontario L2A 5X3

Want to try two free books from another series?
Call 1-800-873-8635 or visit www.ReaderService.com.

* Terms and prices subject to change without notice. Prices do not include applicable
taxes. Sales tax applicable in N.Y. Canadian residents will be charged applicable taxes.
Offer not valid in Quebec. This offer is limited to one order per household. Not valid
for current subscribers to Love Inspired Historical books. All orders subject to credit
approval. Credit or debit balances in a customer's account(s) may be offset by any other
outstanding balance owed by or to the customer. Please allow 4 to 6 weeks for delivery.
Offer available while quantities last.

Your Privacy—The Harlequin® Reader Service is committed to protecting your
privacy. Our Privacy Policy is available online at www.ReaderService.com or upon
request from the Harlequin Reader Service.

We make a portion of our mailing list available to reputable third parties that offer
products we believe may interest you. If you prefer that we not exchange your name with
third parties, or if you wish to clarify or modify your communication preferences, please
visit us at www.ReaderService.com/consumerschoice or write to us at Harlequin Reader
Service Preference Service, P.O. Box 9062, Buffalo, NY 14269. Include your complete
name and address.

LIHDIR13R

ReaderService.com

Manage your account online!

- Review your order history
- Manage your payments
- Update your address

*We've designed
the Harlequin® Reader Service
website just for you.*

Enjoy all the features!

- Reader excerpts from any series
- Respond to mailings and special monthly offers
- Discover new series available to you
- Browse the Bonus Bucks catalog
- Share your feedback

Visit us at:
ReaderService.com